POWDER BURN

Center Point
Large Print

Also by Bradford Scott and available from Center Point Large Print:

The Slick-Iron Trail
Texas Rider

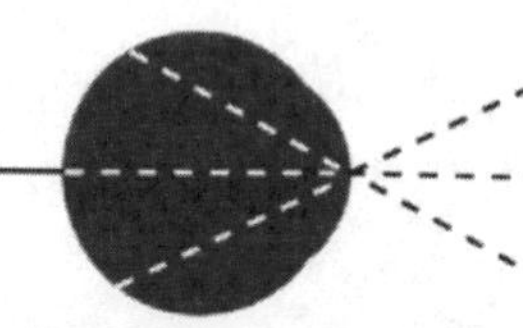

This Large Print Book carries the
Seal of Approval of N.A.V.H.

POWDER BURN

A WALT SLADE WESTERN

Bradford Scott

CENTER POINT LARGE PRINT
THORNDIKE, MAINE

This Center Point Large Print edition
is published in the year 2018 by arrangement with
Golden West Literary Agency.

First US edition: Pyramid Books

The text of this Large Print edition is unabridged.
In other aspects, this book may vary
from the original edition.
Printed in the United States of America
on permanent paper.
Set in 16-point Times New Roman type.

ISBN: 978-1-68324-998-6 (hardcover)
ISBN: 978-1-64358-002-9 (paperback)

Library of Congress Cataloging-in-Publication Data

Names: Scott, Bradford, 1893-1975, author.
Title: Powder burn / Bradford Scott.
Description: Center Point Large Print edition. | Thorndike, Maine : Center Point Large Print, 2018. | Series: A Walt Slade western
Identifiers: LCCN 2018037308| ISBN 9781683249986 (hardcover : alk. paper) | ISBN 9781643580029 (paperback : alk. paper)
Subjects: LCSH: Texas Rangers. | Murder—Investigation. | Large type books.
Classification: LCC PS3537.C9265 P69 2018 | DDC 813/.52—dc23
LC record available at https://lccn.loc.gov/2018037308

ONE

"SHADOW, EITHER I'M SEEING THINGS, or somebody is plain loco!"

Ranger Walt Slade pulled his great black horse to a halt on the crest of a rise and saw more than a mile distant the tawny flood of the Rio Grande where it rolled toward the dark mouth of the Grand Canyon of Santa Helena. The River of the Palms was on a rampage and was decidedly not the proverbial "mile wide and a foot deep, too thick to drink and too thin to plow!"

But it was not the swirling yellow water that held Slade's attention, it was an object that dipped and bobbed on its surface.

"For the love of Pete!" the astounded ranger swore aloud. "Do those jiggers aim to go into the canyon?"

Shadow nodded his head as much as to say that it certainly looked that way.

It looked that way to Slade, too. The men handling the oars, or rather sweeps, of the big flat-bottomed, blunt-prowed boat were apparently not trying to reach either shore. They were holding the craft to the channel, some three hundred yards out from the right bank, and heading straight for the canyon.

In addition to the four men handling the

sweeps, Slade could make out some six or seven more crouched in the boat. But what interested the ranger most was that she undoubtedly carried cargo, other than human freight. She was low in the water from the weight of something, just what he could not at that distance define, which was heaped in a mound that barely allowed the oarsmen space to operate.

Slade's hand tightened on the bridle, but he immediately relaxed again. He could not hope to reach the river bank before the craft would vanish between the canyon walls. Also he had a strong feeling that his intrusion would not be welcome. And he would provide a very nice target as he rode over the ridges, clearly outlined against the sky.

In addition to the hazards of a physical nature, there was a rather touchy question of international law involved, the Rio Grande being the borderline between the United States and Mexico.

Just the same Slade itched to get a close look at what the boat was carrying. He very strongly suspected its nature. He strained his eyes toward the objects in question which appeared to be of considerable length and wrapped in sacking of some sort.

The boat swept on toward a cluster of small buttes and chimney rocks which flanked the towering cliff that was the right wall of the canyon mouth. The craft was almost opposite this miniature badlands when, from the shadow of a butte, mushroomed a puff of whitish smoke. Before he heard the report of the rifle shot, Slade saw one of the oarsmen throw up his hands and pitch sideways over the boat's near gunwale to vanish beneath the swirling water.

As Slade again tightened his hand on the bridle, more puffs spurted from the shadow of the butte. The shots were answered by a volley from the boat. Another oarsman went down, kicking, and the remaining two dropped their sweeps and dived behind the mound of freight. The crackling of the guns reached Slade's ears like the snapping of thorns burning under a briskly boiling pot.

"Trail, Shadow!" he shouted. "That shooting was done in Texas!"

The tall horse shot forward. Like a streak of dark smoke he thundered down the sag but before he got into his full stride the oarless boat, spouting smoke and flame, hurtled past the chimney rocks and into the mouth of the canyon. Instantly the answering shots from the rocks ceased. As Slade neared the bottom of the sag, half a dozen horsemen shot from the shadow of the rocks, curved around the outcropping and went racing east, accompanied by two riderless horses. By the time the ranger pulled his blowing mount to a halt at the base of the butte they had disappeared amid the thick chaparral growth that grew up to the canyon rim.

Knowing that pursuit was hopeless, Slade sat staring at the two sprawled figures beside the rocks, his glance lifting from time to time toward the distant chaparral, which divulged nothing of movement. Satisfied that the killers had kept riding, he dismounted and gave the bodies a careful going-over.

One of the dead men was without doubt a Mexican of much Indian blood. His dark contorted face was blotched and bloated by dissipation and vice. He was stringy in build almost to a state of emaciation. His companion was blocky, powerful-looking, with hard-lined features and pale blue eyes already beginning to glaze. His mouth was a tight streak across his face and even in death was clamped tight. His hair was sandy and sparse. Slade thought it was hard to tell which of the two was the ornerier looking.

Continuing his investigation, Slade began turning out the pockets of the unsavory pair. He discarded, as of no significance, the miscellany of odds and ends the Mexican had but paused suddenly as he came upon a roll of gold pieces neatly packeted. He counted the coin and it added up to two hundred dollars. This gent had been doing quite well by himself of late.

A moment later, Slade whistled through his teeth when the other man's pockets disgorged a similar roll of gold which also totalled two hundred dollars. Holding the money in the palm of his bronzed hand, he stared at the rushing water.

It looks like a payoff, he mused. The men had gotten paid in advance for a chore they were elected to do, and it was logical to assume that the chore was to stop the boat.

Well, they didn't stop it, but they did send it into the canyon, which, in Slade's opinion, amounted to the same thing. The flat-bottomed scow would be under water before it covered a third of the way through the awful gorge. Of course, the boatmen may have intended to slant across to the south bank just above the canyon, but it sure didn't look that way. True, they were in the channel and breasting the full sweep of the current, but even with the river running as it was, four men at the oars would have been able to make the south shore. But to all appearances they were making no such effort. The prow of the boat was pointing downstream and it certainly looked like they were aiming straight for the Santa Helena.

It just didn't seem to make sense. Nobody but a lunatic would try to shoot the rapids in the middle and lower canyon. It had been done by a few explorers with specially constructed boats and elaborate equipment and safeguards. And even those intrepid adventurers admitted that before they were through the gorge they wished heartily that they had never started on such a fool's errand. That an unwieldy scow could expect to make the hazardous passage unscathed was rankest nonsense.

"But darn it, horse, they were headed into that infernal canyon," he told Shadow. He gazed across the tawny flood to Mexico. "And anyhow I'm willing to bet that those jiggers in the boat were part of Sebastian Cavorca's bunch. That old hellion would charge on the devil with a bucket of water and I reckon some of his lack of fear rubs off on anybody associated with him. In fact, I've a notion the only idea of fear old Cavorca ever had was his murky interpretation of the dictionary definition of the word, if he ever looked inside a dictionary."

Shadow did not appear overly impressed by the argument and tossed his head sideways in general disagreement.

In his own mind Slade was convinced that the boat had been one of Cavorca's smuggling outfits, although where they hoped to land their cargo in a stretch of country constantly patrolled by the *rurales*, the Mexican mounted police, was past understanding.

More interesting, although just as unanswerable, was who would be sent to stop them, from the north side of the river? The possible answer to that one intrigued Slade greatly. Was somebody bucking Cavorca? If so, that unknown individual would be somebody to reckon with.

His glance returned to the dead men, but they were in no condition to answer questions. He went over the bodies again, tearing out the lining of pockets, turning hatbands, even removing boots and carefully scrutinizing heels and soles for possible cunningly concealed hiding places. With a disgusted growl, he gave up. Well, he'd report the matter to the sheriff of the county, with whom he had an appointment at the mining town of Tule more than twenty miles to the east. The coroner could ride down and look the bodies over if he was of a mind to. They'd keep. No self-respecting coyote or buzzard would touch them.

The two rifles lying near the slain pair interested Slade. They were Winchester repeaters of the latest model, excellent weapons and brand new. He wondered where the unsavory-looking pair had gotten them. They were rather unusual for such Border scum to be packing.

Not wishing to be encumbered with the arms on the long ride ahead of him, he laid them beside the bodies. The gold, however, he dropped into his saddle pouch. He'd turn that over to the sheriff. No sense in leaving it here for some chance wanderer to tie onto. He wondered why the other drygulchers didn't take the money before departing, but a moment's reflection offered an obvious explanation. Seeing him riding down the slope and not knowing who he was or whether he had companions following, they had thought it best to hightail without delay, doubtless forgetting all about the large sum their slain companions were carrying. With a last look around, he mounted Shadow and rode to the crest of a nearby ridge from which he could get his bearings.

The man the peons of the Rio Grande River villages, who looked upon him as the tried and tested friend of the lowly people, had named El Halcon—The Hawk, made a striking picture outlined against the hard blue of the Texas sky. More than six feet tall, his breadth of shoulders and girth of chest matched his height. His lean, deeply-bronzed face was dominated by cold, reckless gray eyes that seemed to have little devils of laughter dancing in their depths, the eyes of one who knows that the world is full of jest for those who can see the springs that work it. His rather wide mouth, grin-quirked at the corners, somewhat relieved the touch of fierceness evinced by the prominent, high-bridged nose above and the powerful chin and jaw beneath. His pushed back "J.B." revealed crisp hair so black that a blue shadow seemed to lie upon it.

Slade wore the homely garb of a rider of the purple sage—faded overalls and blue shirt, vivid neckerchief about his sinewy throat, a broad-brimmed gray "rain-shed" much the worse for wear, and high-heeled half boots of softly-tanned leather. About his lean waist were double cartridge belts from the carefully worked and oiled cut-out holsters of which protruded the plain black butts of heavy guns. And from those guns' handles his slender bronzed hands seemed never far away. In the saddle boot under his left thigh was snugged a heavy Winchester repeating rifle.

He was universally respected and admired by honest men who knew him to be a Texas Ranger. The smartest, ablest and most fearless of the rangers, they said, and that was saying a good deal. But because he sometimes worked under cover and didn't reveal his ranger connections, there were others, including some puzzled peace officers, who declared that if El Halcon wasn't an owlhoot, he missed being one by the width of a frog's hair. They would complain, "Nobody can ever get anything on the hellion. Sure he's got killings to his credit, but somehow whenever he cashes somebody in, it turns out the hellion has a killing coming. So what in blazes are you going to do?"

By those of the far-flung outlaw brotherhood of the great state who knew him to be a ranger, he was hated and feared. And by those who knew him as El Halcon of dubious reputation he was also hated and feared. "The blasted lone wolf is always horning in on somebody else's good thing, skimming off the cream and lining his own pockets!" they would wrathfully declare. "And anybody who tangles with him ends pushing up the daisies. Looks like the bullet ain't run that can kill the devil, and if he hasn't got the fastest gunhand in Texas, the gent who has is sure keeping under cover. He's one of those sidewinders you see once in a blue moon—a two-gun man who pulls with either hand and shoots with either hand. He don't pack that second gun as a reserve, as most double artillery wearing jiggers do. He's just as liable to pull with his left hand as with his right, and each one is as fast and accurate as the other. And he manages to hypnotize sheriffs and other hellions of that sort. Sooner or later he has 'em eating out of his hand."

So the story went, but of late a whisper was running along the Texas-Mexico Border, "If he ever tangles with Murray De Spain, then we'll see!"

Slade gazed speculatively to the northeast where Cigar Mountain loomed against the sky, then shifted his glance eastward from the great peak toward Study Butte, a misty shadow, where quicksilver had been mined for many years. Chief of the mines was the old Chisos, but some twelve or fourteen other mines had been opened since its discovery. Mexicans living in primitive fashion found employment in the mines. The whole section had been easy going and peaceful until less than a year before. Then gold had been discovered in the hills between Cigar Mountain and Study Butte and since then there had been little peace and less quiet, especially in the mining town of Tule.

Slade had a fair notion that Tule was where the men who had drygulched the boat were heading when they left in such a hurry. Perhaps he would learn something in the mining town. With a last glance at the bodies and the turbulent river he rode north by east.

The sun was low in the west before Slade reached Tule. Almost due east, he could see the vast bulk of the Chisos Mountains flaming red, purple and yellow, a rainbow of vivid color outlined against the sky. There was a contemplative look in Slade's gray eyes as he gazed at the great upheaval shimmering with a fiery glow. The misty appearing "phantoms" were hole-in-the-wall country and a favorite hangout for gentlemen with unsavory pasts and presents and unpredictable futures. Quite likely, he thought, the bunch he saw ride away from the river were headed eventually for the Chisos, but he was of the opinion that they would stop off at Tule. He wished he had been close enough to get a good look at them. Well, something might happen in

Tule that would give him a line-up on them, and through them perhaps a line-up on a gentleman he very much wanted to meet face to face.

Something would happen, all right, and Ranger Walt Slade, to his not unqualified delight, would be in the middle of it.

TWO

THE TEXAS BIG BEND COUNTRY was a sparsely settled region, but a gold strike could increase the population of a section astonishingly. Such was the case with Tule, which was considerably larger than the county seat and boasted enough inhabitants to make things more than lively, especially along the crooked main street. In fact, Sheriff John Horton kept three deputies stationed there and was himself a frequent visitor.

When he reached the town, Slade's first thought was for his horse. He located a livery stable without difficulty and gave Shadow into the care of a peg-legged gentleman with bristling black hair and whiskers liberally streaked with gray, frosty blue eyes and a truculent look.

However, without waiting to be formally introduced, something usually necessary before a stranger could put a hand on the big black, he rubbed Shadow's nose, swore at him jovially and had the rig off before Slade could reach for it.

"He'll be right here when you want him," he promised the ranger. "I got a Sharps buffalo gun easy on the trigger that says so. Place to sleep? Got a room over the stalls, right alongside the one I pound my ear in. Don't often rent it, but a gent who forks a horse like this one is bound to be okay. Here's a key to the front door when you stagger in around daybreak, like chuck line riders always do after they hit town. You can wash up at the trough in back. Clean running water and there's soap and a towel. Try not to fall up the stairs when you come in; I sleep light. The Root Hog saloon? Right on Main Street two streets east from this one. You been here before?"

"I was through this way a couple of years back but I don't recall seeing the place," Slade explained.

"Wasn't here then," the stablekeeper replied. "Town's perked up considerable since they struck gold in the hills. Lots of new places. Some big *cantinas* in the Mexican quarter up at the east end of Main Street. Good music in 'em, and nice looking *señoritas* who are willing to be friendly."

Slade left the stable chuckling, and confident that Shadow was in good hands. He located the Root Hog, which proved to be a big combination saloon and restaurant. He pushed through the swinging doors, paused and glanced about. Almost immediately he spotted a quiet, mild-mannered and elderly gentleman with almost white hair and a short beard streaked with gray sitting alone at a corner table and smoking a cigar. He looked more like a benign church deacon than what he was, the tough sheriff of a tough county about the size of an average eastern state. Folks said that a six-shooter and a Bible were Sheriff

John Horton's constant companions, and that he was equally adept with either.

The sheriff raised his hand and beckoned. Slade crossed the room and sat down opposite the peace officer who regarded him in silence for a moment.

"Well," he said at length, "find out anything?"

"Not much, but perhaps more than I realized," Slade replied. "I'll tell you what happened. Anything new with you?"

The sheriff shook his head. "Just the same old story," he answered. "We're watching this whole section of the Border as best we can, with some little help from the customs people. Not much from them, they've got their hands full farther east, around Laredo and Brownsville and Port Isabel. On the Mexican side of the Rio Grande, Governor Alvarez has his *rurales* strung along the river wherever there's a chance for stuff to come through. *El Presidente* sent up a detachment of regulars from Mexico City to give Alvarez a hand and they are on the job, but the stuff keeps getting through. Sebastian Cavorca is a smooth old scoundrel if there ever was one, and he has built up an organization that's a beaut. He has every owl-hoot, peon-beater and other scallywag in Chihuahua back of him, and he's already spreading over into Sonora to the west and Coahuila to the east. All he needs is plenty of rifles and ammunition to arm his varmints and he'll win the election month after next hands down. Then as governor of Chihuahua again and with the spadework already done in the other states, before the year is out he'll have his own men controlling the local governments in Sonora and Coahuila and be all set for a full-fledged revolution. *El Presidente* realizes the danger and is giving Governor Alvarez all the help he can, but he's got troubles of his own in other sections and hasn't many men to spare. No wonder Alvarez is fit to be roped."

Slade nodded. He already knew all the sheriff had outlined. "And if this thing really gets out of hand, there'll be trouble a-plenty along the Texas Border, which is what the rangers are alarmed about," he said gravely. "Mexico needs a change in government, but not the kind of change Sebastian Cavorca would give it. The time will come when somebody will arise down there, somebody from the people, and will really clean house. Then they'll have a government like ours, really of the people. It will come, with trouble and bloodshed, but not by way of the Cavorca sort. From him both Mexico and Texas would get nothing but trouble and bloodshed."

"I think you're right," replied the sheriff. "Governor Alvarez is a square-shooter, an honest man and tries to do what's right. When he upset old Cavorca and got elected governor he cleaned house in his state for fair, kicked out all the

Cavorca bunch of sidewinders and replaced them with decent people. Naturally the Cavorca bunch didn't like it and is trying to get the upper hand again."

"And with Cavorca having Murray De Spain to help him up here, they're likely to do it unless we bust up the De Spain smuggling ring," Slade declared with conviction.

Sheriff Horton gave the Ranger a curious glance. "You're still convinced there's such a man as Murray De Spain, then?"

"There is," Slade replied grimly. "Oh, I know he's regarded almost as a legend, an owlhoot build-up, but he exists, all right. And he's even more than the yarns about him say. I've been trailing him, or trying to, for months now, and I know all the stories told of him are a long ways from being just grasshopper library stuff. I saw him once and I'll never forget him."

"You really have seen him?" Horton asked with interest. "That's more than most folks up here can say. What does he look like?"

"Just about the finest looking man I ever saw," Slade returned. "Big, straight as an Indian, with curly yellow hair, perfect features and twinkling blue eyes. Yes, just the finest looking jigger I ever laid eyes on."

Sheriff Horton contemplated his table companion and wondered if the young ranger had ever taken the trouble to glance into a mirror.

"They say he's from Tennessee," Slade continued. "A gentleman in the beginning, no doubt. Folks say he's a college man, a black sheep member of a fine old family. Had a row with his people and went bad. Been all over the world and has done most everything. Helped Paramont and Bellares stage their revolution in Peru. Got out alive when the revolutionaries were routed by the government troops and Paramont and Bellares were caught and hanged. Got out by way of trails over the Andes Mountains. Folks said that had never been done before. There are plenty who will tell you he's got the fastest gunhand in the Southwest, and the most accurate. I'm inclined to believe them. Usually goes masked. I've a notion, though, I'd know him again, masked or unmasked, if I got a good look at his right hand."

"How's that?" the sheriff asked.

"Well, the time I saw him was when he and his bunch tried to hold up the mail train just west of Del Rio," Slade explained. "He and I went for our hardware and he lost the end of his middle finger. I've still got the gun he pulled. Had the smashed butt-plate replaced and kept it as a souvenir. Never carried it. I don't like pearl handles—too slippery."

Sheriff Horton smiled in his beard. " 'Fastest gunhand in the Southwest'," he quoted, under his breath, Slade's previous remark apropos of Murray De Spain.

Slade's hearing was uncannily keen and he chuckled. "De Spain was just turning around and he didn't really get set or the story might have had a different ending."

"Maybe," conceded the sheriff without conviction. "He got away?"

"That's right," Slade agreed. "They got to their horses, except one who stayed behind. I was riding the train with my horse in a boxcar in the rear. The cashed-in jigger they left behind was an ornery-looking specimen."

Sheriff Horton smiled again and Slade chuckled.

"That little incident was a first rate example of De Spain's shrewdness and how he operates—he's just like a will-o-the-wisp, here, there and everywhere, except where he's supposed to be. I'd gotten what I considered perfectly reliable information that he'd pulled out of the Port Isabel section where he had been operating and was in the Big Bend country. So I took the train west, and ran smack into him nearly two hundred miles east of where he was supposed to be. Liable as not he's sitting behind us right now, disguised, listening to our conversation."

Sheriff Horton hastily glanced over his shoulder but observed nothing more threatening than a harmless old Mexican eating a bowl of chili. He turned back to Slade and risked a chuckle of his own.

"I believe you said you have something to tell me," he reminded.

Slade nodded agreement and gave him an account of what he had witnessed at the canyon mouth.

"And the stuff in the boat appeared to be wrapped in sacking," he concluded. "Rifles and ammunition are my guess."

"I'm inclined to agree with you," said the sheriff. "The mule loads we intercepted last month were wrapped in burlap. A small train, just six mules, but they were loaded heavy."

"You took no prisoners?" Slade asked.

"That's right," answered the sheriff. "When the riders saw us coming they abandoned the mules and hightailed. We couldn't catch up with them. The hellions had mighty good horses. And you saw the boat go into the canyon? Well, that's one load Cavorca won't get. No boat like you described could live through the Santa Helena."

Slade rolled a cigarette and lighted it. For some minutes he smoked in silence. "Sheriff," he said at length, "I wonder. Could they by any chance run the stuff by way of the canyon?"

Sheriff Horton laughed aloud. "Why, son," he replied, "that canyon is fifteen to eighteen hundred feet deep. Only a few loco explorers have ever managed to get through, and they had boats built to order for the purpose and life rafts and other special equipment. You must know that. Rock slides and rapids make navigation through the canyon practically impossible. No old flat-bottom could stay afloat for a third of the fifteen miles to the south mouth."

"But suppose," Slade persisted, "they didn't try to go all the way through but tied up someplace north of the rapids and sent the stuff up the far wall? I understand there are game trails up the walls, particularly on the Mexican side. I've a notion a man could go up by way of some of those trails."

"Reckon I know as much about those trails as anybody," the sheriff said. "I'll agree that an active man might scramble up from the river by way of them, but not packing a load of rifles and ammunition. That would be impossible."

"Mules and burros are mighty sure-footed critters," Slade remarked.

"Agreed," said the sheriff, "but nobody could persuade mules or burros to go down the trails there—they know what's safe and won't tackle anything they consider isn't. And even if you could get them to go down they couldn't get out again, loaded. Goats could do it, I reckon, but you can't pack that sort of a load on a goat's back."

"I reckon you're right," Slade admitted, "but it sure looked to me like that boat was deliberately heading for the canyon. It's sure, too, that they couldn't have gotten the stuff past the patrols north or south of the canyon. I suppose the stretch bordering the canyon isn't patrolled on the south side."

"Nor on the north side, either," grunted the sheriff. "We've got mighty few men on this side, certainly none to waste where there isn't a chance of the stuff going across, and the same goes for the Mexicans to the south. They've got a lot more than we have, but none they don't need. You won't find any wasting time on that crack in the ground.

"But the hellions are getting through somehow," he added with a growl. "And if they keep on at the rate they're going, Sebastian Cavorca is going to end up the big skookum he-wolf below the line."

"And," Slade stated, "if he does get control of the Mexican government, Murray De Spain will be telling him what to do and showing him how to do it. That is, till he decides to take over himself," he added grimly.

"Good Lord!" snorted the sheriff. "Do you really believe that, Slade?"

"I do," Slade said flatly.

Sheriff Horton swore wearily. "The way you say it, you make me half believe it, crazy sounding as it is," he grumbled. "And if your blasted Murray De Spain really is, and is what folks say he is, I reckon I'll have to believe it."

Slade chuckled as he managed to unscramble

the last sentence. “Let’s eat,” he suggested. They proceeded to do so.

Finally Sheriff Horton drained a last cup of coffee, lighted a cigar and stood up.

“I’m going to turn in,” he announced. “Didn’t get much sleep last night. See you in the morning. You going to bed?”

“I think I’ll scout around a little first and look the town over,” Slade replied. “Appears to have grown considerably since I was here two years ago.”

“It has, and for the worse,” growled the sheriff. “So long!”

Slade sat smoking for some time after the sheriff departed. Then, satisfied there was nothing to be learned in the Root Hog, he too left the saloon.

Strolling along the main street, he dropped into place after place, lingering a while in each, listening to random talk at the bars and games, scanning faces. Gradually as the evening wore on toward midnight, with no abatement of Tule’s noise and turbulence, he worked into the quarter where the Mexican quicksilver miners lived. This was the old original portion of the town and here the scene was radically different. Spanish was spoken much more than English. Black velvet and silver *conchas* took the place of corduroys and overalls. Chattering groups stood on the street corners. Dark-haired *señoritas* drifted past, flashing oblique, bright-eyed glances at the tall ranger. Peons in hempen sandals, serapes and huge steeple-sombreros shuffled along. There was a sprinkling of lithe vaqueros, the Mexican cowhands. An occasional waddie from the ranches to the east bow-legged his way through the crowd, batwing chaps flaring out from his thighs, vivid neckerchief about his throat. Strolling troubadours with mandolin or guitar passed in and out of the *cantinas*.

Something after midnight, Slade paused before a rather larger and more ornate *cantina* than those farther down the street. Across the window was legended "La Rosalita."

Slade recalled Sheriff Horton mentioning the place as being run by one Tomas Garcia, a fat man with a bland smile that never quite reached his heavy-lidded eyes. Garcia, the sheriff said, was suspected of engaging in activities less innocent than the running of a drinking establishment, but nothing had ever been proven against him.

Slade hesitated an instant, then entered the place. It was rather dimly lighted by two big hanging lamps, one over the bar, the other above the center of the dance floor. The shadows clustering about the roof beams and in the corners lent a sinister air to the room that was accentuated by the shivery wail of muted violins and the soft liquid notes of guitars.

The corpulent individual presiding at the far

end of the bar was, Slade decided, Tomas Garcia. Assisting him were three bartenders, hard-faced, alert men whose eyes seemed to miss nothing. The same applied to the dealers at the games and the waiters padding about. Slade felt that La Rosalita was a rather interesting place.

Nobody appeared to pay him any particular notice. He made his way across the room and sat down behind a table close to the wall. From this point of vantage he had a good view of all that went on around him. He ordered a drink and as he sat sipping it his keen ears gathered in scraps of conversation. Mostly Spanish was spoken, which Slade understood perfectly. He had a feeling that most anything was likely to happen in Garcia's place.

A red-lipped dance-floor girl weaved past his table with seductively swaying hips. Slade met her gaze but smilingly shook his head when she glanced suggestively at a vacant chair. He was not averse to feminine companionship but tonight his mind was too filled with weighty problems to be open to light banter or soft whisperings. And he wished to avoid distraction of any kind. The feeling that anything might happen here was growing stronger.

For some time he sat listening and watching, allowing the waiter to refill his glass from time to time, and neither heard nor saw anything of outstanding interest. Then, during a lull in the music, a troubador strolled in strumming his guitar. He was tall, the breadth of his shoulders and the narrowness of his waist accentuated by his elaborate and tight-fitting costume. A silken scarf was wound about his head, gypsy style, completely covering his hair, the tasselled ends hanging down the back of his flowered and braided jacket. His ornate sombrero, heavily crusted with silver, was drawn low over his eyes. A handkerchief of flame-colored silk muffled his throat almost to the chin, so that little could be seen between hat-brim and neckerchief save a straight nose, a square chin and a gleam of eyes. He glanced toward the orchestra leader inquiringly, got a nod of acquiescence and walked lithely to the middle of the dance floor. With a sudden flash of white teeth he struck a booming chord on his guitar and began to sing, in a pure, sweet tenor, a love song of old Spain.

Abruptly the babble of conversation was hushed. Walt Slade, called by many "the singingest man in Texas," straightened in his chair. The troubador's voice was decidedly out of the ordinary. Very quickly the whole attention of the room was centered on him.

People began pushing in from the street, attracted by the unusual quality of the impromptu entertainment. Unnoticed in the jostling crowd, a number of dark-faced men with keen, watchful eyes drifted into the room by ones and twos.

While appearing to wander aimlessly about, they took up strategic positions and with singular intentness centered their attention on the singer.

So entertained the unusual troubador, Walt Slade for once failed to note what was going on around him. He did not see the furtive newcomers move about the room.

The singer's eyes gazed straight ahead—straight toward where Tomas Garcia stood with both fat hands outspread on the bar. Without the slightest preliminary warning, his voice snapped off in the middle of a verse. Again it rang through the room, all the music gone from it, hard and cold as frosted steel, as the dropped guitar thudded on the floor, "Tomas Garcia!"

The *cantina* owner straightened up as if jerked erect by a hidden wire. The singer's hand flashed to his belt, came up in a move too swift for the eye to follow. At the same instant his other hand swept the sombrero and scarf aside, revealing curling golden hair and blazing blue eyes.

Garcia screamed, a harsh choking scream, terrible in its terror. Across the room darted a lance of light to center on Garcia's throat. He fell forward, clawing at the bar, over which spouted a torrent of blood from the gaping knife wound in his throat.

A split second before the room fairly exploded with gunfire, Walt Slade's amazed ejaculation shattered the stunned silence, "Murray De Spain!"

THREE

DE SPAIN'S EARS WERE SHARP AS A DOG'S. He whirled at the sound of Slade's voice. His eyes flamed with recognition.

"El Halcon!" he yelled. "Blast you—" With the same effortless ease with which he drew and hurled the knife, he whipped a gun from his belt. Slade's hand flashed down and up.

But before either could pull trigger a squalling Mexican, his ear bullet-nicked, and glaring wildly back over his shoulder as he fled, barged full into Slade's table. Down went Mexican, table, chairs and Ranger in a screeching, crackling, cursing tangle. Into the wall thudded De Spain's bullet. Over the ruin of furniture and the sprawling bodies of Slade and the Mexican swept the panic-stricken crowd.

Two of Garcia's bartenders were down. The third was staggering about, shot to pieces, dying on his feet. Two dealers and a waiter were dead. Those remaining on their feet were shooting in every direction.

Murray De Spain's gun muzzle tipped up, flashed fire. The lamp over the dance floor snuffed out and splintered glass rained on the floor. De Spain spun around, fired again. Out went the lamp over the bar. Black darkness covered the room like a blanket.

Slade got the Mexican by the nape of the neck and hurled him out of the way. He started to scramble to his feet and was immediately knocked to the floor again as somebody catapulted over his back. Still gripping his gun, he grabbed a chair rung with his left hand and flailed about him. Another moment and he was on his feet, fighting his way to the door. As he neared it he heard a clatter of fast hoofs outside.

"Made their getaway, blast them!" he swore. "Talk about team work! Better than a prime cuttin' horse and a rope!"

By sheer strength he bored his way through the throng of terror-stricken humanity and bulged through the door. Outside was a rioting pandemonium, men fighting to get in the clear, others fighting to get nearer the scene of excitement. Inside the *cantina* things were still a mite more than mild. Guns were banging, furniture smashing, voices bawling curses. A reddish glow ominously framed the window panes. Evidently oil from the bullet-punctured lamps had caught fire. Somebody came through a window with a terrific clang-jangling of smashed glass and splintered woodwork. Others followed. More windows went to pieces. The front door was vomiting a steady stream.

Slade shouldered his way to a comparatively

clear space. He gazed speculatively at the burning building. It looked like everybody would get out save Garcia and a few of his hellions, and the chances were they wouldn't mind a little more fire where they'd gone if there was any justice in Creation. And as the building sat off by itself nothing else would be likely to catch.

"I'm a peace officer and supposed to keep order," he muttered, "but what's needed here is the warden of a lunatic asylum! To heck with it!"

Glancing along the street, which was now brilliantly lighted by the flames of the burning building, he observed Sheriff Horton in a state of half-dress hurrying forward, his three deputies at his heels. Slade moved to intercept them.

"Hold it," he advised. "No sense in getting mixed up in that hullabaloo. Might start off something else. They'll quiet down by themselves very quickly now. These people are excitable but naturally peaceful. They're all good hard-working folks and respect authority. Wait a few minutes and then let your deputies saunter around and talk to them. The real trouble-makers are either dead or gone away from here."

"But what in blazes started it all?" demanded the sheriff.

Slade told him what happened in *La Rosalita*. "Tonight we've had a little example of how Murray De Spain works," Slade concluded. "What do you think of him now?"

"I'm beginning to think he's everything you said of him and more," the sheriff growled. "But why the blazes did he kill Garcia?"

"I think the answer to that is fairly obvious," Slade replied. "I believe you told me Garcia had been suspected of being mixed up in smuggling activities for a long time. Perhaps he thought De Spain was trespassing on his preserves. I'm convinced now it was Garcia who staged the raid on the boat. De Spain either knew or heard it was Garcia and set out to even up the score in his own nice little way, at the same time removing Garcia from the picture as a potential nuisance."

"You may be right," conceded the sheriff. "I'll admit I've been leaning to the notion that it was Garcia who was smuggling the arms to Cavorca, but maybe you've got the straight of it and it is De Spain. The nerve of that sidewinder! Coming to town and pulling a killing and starting a riot right under my nose. I wish you'd managed to line sights with him."

"Looked like he was more apt to line sights with me," Slade answered. "I figured he had the jump on me and would have gotten in the first shot. Reckon that scared-loco Mexican with half an ear saved me from getting an airhole in my hide. As it was I felt the wind of the slug De Spain sent at me. But I got stomped on more than a cow-poke under a stampede. I've a notion my back looks like the Chihuahua Trail on a busy day."

"However, maybe some good came out of the ruckus," he added. "Now I'm absolutely certain it was De Spain's bunch handling that boat and that they were headed into the Santa Helena. And just as convinced it's possible to reach Mexico by way of that infernal canyon."

"You're probably right about the boat being manned by some of De Spain's bunch," conceded the sheriff, "but I still can't see them transporting the stuff to Mexico by way of the canyon. Nothing can live in that hole. Why, birds have been known to starve to death in there. Get in and can't get out again, because of the down draughts, I reckon. Nope, I just can't go along with you on the theory that the boat was deliberately heading into the canyon. I figure the hellions intended to cut across right above the canyon, maybe having information that there was no patrol active there right then. The attack on them caused them to go into the canyon and by now their bodies are halfway to the Gulf of Mexico."

"No sense in arguing about it," Slade said, "but I still think I'm right and I intend to try and find out."

"Go to it," said the sheriff. "You're the ranger as well as Captain McNelty's lieutenant and ace-man. I'm just a sheriff with lots of headaches. Looks like things are quieting down. Okay, boys," he told the deputies, "mosey around and suggest to folks it might be a good notion to go home and go to bed. That's what I'm going to do right now. Oh, by the way, Slade, do you think De Spain has you spotted as a ranger?"

"I don't think so," Slade replied. "He knows me as El Halcon and very likely considers me a rival owlhoot planning to horn in on his pickings. Not that it would make any particular difference. He'd just as soon kill a ranger as anybody else, if the ranger got in his way."

"Plumb snake-blooded, eh?"

"He's all of that," Slade agreed. "And smarter than any snake that ever slid a scale. A snake is usually a flatheaded ignoramus and that description certainly doesn't apply to Murray De Spain."

"Hope he tries to get through that canyon and drowns himself," growled the sheriff. "Well, now I am going to bed."

He lumbered off. Slade watched him pass beyond the ring of firelight and turned his attention back to his immediate surroundings.

The crowd was thinning out. The three deputies strolled about, speaking a word here and there. When the fire had died down sufficiently, they would poke about in the ashes and try to ascertain how many had died in the ruckus and an inquest would be held over whatever remains were not totally cremated. Slade decided he'd had enough excitement for one day and went to bed.

He slept till mid-morning and then repaired to the Root Hog for some breakfast. In the saloon the row of the night before was the chief topic of conversation and many wild guesses were hazarded as to the reason for it. The general opinion was that it had been a falling out between two outlaw bunches, Garcia evidently having belonged to one, something that had been suspected for some time. Slade heard no mention of smuggling, nor did he hear Murray De Spain's name spoken. It looked like he was the only one who had recognized the legendary outlaw leader. But Slade knew from the curious glances cast in his direction that plenty of Tule folks knew that the notorious El Halcon was in their midst. This, however, gave him little concern. In fact, he felt that it should work to his advantage. He suppressed a grin as a fragment of conversation reached his ears.

"Saw the sheriff talking to him last night," a man at the bar was observing in an undertone to his drinking companion. "Reckon he warned him not to go pulling anything in this section. Wouldn't be surprised if he trails his twine."

"Maybe," the other replied dubiously. "John Horton is a salty old jigger, all right, but he's a plumb stickler for the law and I reckon he knows there ain't no reward notices out for that big jigger. If there was, he wouldn't have just talked to him last night. He'd have clapped him behind bars pronto. You know you can't put a man in jail for what people think about him. Not in this country, thank God! And until Sheriff Horton knows something against El Halcon, he ain't going to tell him to move on just because some folks figure he's an outlaw. Maybe he is, but it ain't been proved, and until it is proved, the Texas way, and the American way, is to give him the benefit of the doubt and figure he ain't."

"Reckon that's so," the other agreed. "And whether he is or whether he ain't, when he grins it's mighty hard not to like the big devil. Never saw a grin change a man's face so. No matter how grumpy you're feeling, you just have to grin back."

The speaker automatically glanced toward the subject of the conversation and Slade did grin. The other turned red, looked awkward and—grinned back. Slade attacked his breakfast with an even heartier appetite than is common to youth and perfect digestion.

FOUR

AFTER EATING, Slade sat for some time deep in thought, trying to make up his mind as to what his next move would be. Finally he arrived at a decision. The smuggler boat had suffered disaster the day before. Was it not logical to believe that the smugglers, having learned caution from the misadventure, would not again attempt a like operation during the daylight hours? Slade believed it was. Under cover of darkness they would have a much better chance to thwart another possible drygulching.

This decided, he left the saloon and visited a general store a little way down the street. Here he purchased some staple provisions and repaired to the livery stable where he had left his horse. He stowed the food in his saddle pouches beside a small skillet and a little flat bucket that were always there and got the rig on Shadow.

"Expect to see you again tomorrow," he told the stable keeper after settling Shadow's account. He mounted the big black and rode out of town, headed east toward the rangeland farther on that accommodated several big ranches. He rode at a moderate pace until he was out of sight of the town, then he spoke to Shadow and sent him along the trail at top speed for better than a mile, finally slackening his pace where the trail wound through a long stretch of dense and high chaparral.

"If we were wearing a tail when we left town, I figure we should have lost it," he told the black as he veered him into the growth and headed due south.

The belt was a little more than half a mile thick and they eventually reached more open country without mishap. Slade continued south for a few more miles, then veered west toward the north mouth of the Santa Helena canyon. He did not push the horse for he had no desire to reach his destination before nightfall. Dusk was falling before he sighted the rugged upheaval that walled the canyon. He did not at once approach the canyon mouth but turned off into a thicket where a little stream ran on its way to join the river. He kindled a small fire of dry wood, confident that the smoke would not show in the deepening dusk, and quickly threw together an appetizing meal. Afterward he smoked beside the fire until it had died to ashes, slipped the bit back into Shadow's mouth, tightened the cinches and mounted. The east was brightening and soon a full moon soared up over the hills and flooded the wild country with a mellow glow in which objects stood out in detail. The river was a shimmer of molten silver and any object on its surface would be clearly outlined.

Reaching the canyon mouth, Slade took up his post on a ridge about three hundred yards distant and waited. He could see for quite a long distance up the river, but landward his view was restricted by other ridges and broken ground and clumps of chaparral, especially to the northwest. To the east the terrain was somewhat more open, the contours flattened.

Hour after dragging hour passed. The moon climbed higher, the light grew more silvery, and the surface of the hurrying water remained unbroken by any alien object. Slade's eyes grew heavy from the constant strain of peering through the luminous gloom and an increasing desire for sleep weighed down his lids. There was something hypnotic in the gliding stream of molten silver splotched with the frostier gleam of ripple crests and the ebon of the hollows between. From time to time he would look away from the river, staring at clumps of chaparral, the sprinkling of stars, even the pale disc of the moon in an effort to relieve his clouded vision.

His tired eyes began to play tricks on him and he seemed to see movement where he knew perfectly well none existed. Clumps of brush appeared to steal stealthily forward. Rocks took on the semblance of crouching men advancing step by slow step, pregnant with menace. One distant bristle of growth became a company of horse poised for the charge. He could have sworn he saw the animals toss impatient heads and strain against the check reins. He swore wearily, rubbed his eyes and wished he dare light a cigarette that would relieve somewhat the steadily mounting tension that was frazzling his nerves to the breaking point.

So often had he been fooled that it took him some seconds to be assured that the dark object breaking the silver monotony of the river was real and not just another delusion of overwrought imagination.

"Shadow, that's the real thing!" he exclaimed exultantly. "Yes, it's a boat. My hunch was a straight one."

On came the craft, hurried along by the current. Slade could make out the figures of men manning the sweeps, others crouching beside a mound of cargo. Again it was an old flatbottom, apparently identical to the one he had seen the day before. He leaned forward eagerly as it neared the black mouth of the canyon.

Then he jerked erect, hurling himself far to the side. Flame had gushed from the boat. A bullet yelled past.

Wrathfully, Slade reached for his own Winchester, but before he could draw it a second slug whistled by his ear, this time from the west. He shot a glance over his shoulder.

Riding toward him and not three hundred yards distant was a group of horsemen who were certainly not moon-witched chaparral. He was caught in a crossfire.

Slade acted instantly. He hunched down over the horse's neck and his voice rang out.

"Trail, Shadow, trail!" he shouted. "Sift sand, horse. Those hellions are real, too!"

The great black shot forward. Slade hunched as low as he could. Bullets whined by, coming from two directions. He felt the burn of one that grazed his cheek. Another ripped the sleeve of his shirt. A third almost knocked his left foot from the stirrup as it sliced off a section of his boot heel. He was on a very hot spot indeed.

But a man hunkered low on a speeding horse is an elusive target in deceptive moonlight. Another moment and he was out of sight of the men in the boat and the horsemen were losing ground as Shadow got into full stride.

For a thousand yards the bullets continued to buzz past like angry hornets, and then they ceased to come. Shadow was steadily increasing the distance of separation; the three hundred yards had increased to more than four and the pursuers were giving all their attention to riding.

Having come through the initial brush unscathed, Slade was now not particularly concerned. Shadow was gaining on the pursuit at every stride and barring an unpredictable accident or a miracle there was scant danger of the following riders running him down. Slade glanced back, contemplated sending a few slugs of his own to enliven the proceedings but decided against it. Better to keep a sharp watch on the trail ahead. The track was rough and stony and a fall at this juncture would be fatal.

"You can handle it from here on," he told Shadow cheerfully. "And we did find out what we came for. Boats do go into that infernal canyon. June along, horse, those gents will give it up before long. Wonder where in blazes they came from, anyhow. Riding parallel to the boat in the water as a guard, the chances are."

And then abruptly he saw something which changed an exhilarating race into something deadly serious.

Charging down from the north was a second band of horsemen riding a long slant that would eventually bring them to the trail ahead of him. He belatedly realized that the bunch behind had not been convoying the boat; they had been patiently waiting behind a distant ridge until his attention was centered on the craft. Then they had ridden from concealment and the shot from the boat was the signal to open the ball. He had gaily ambled into the jaws of a trap.

The strategy was simple and effective. Crowd him against the southern hills, between the two forces, and finish him off. That was all there was to it and unless he thought of something darn fast it was going to work. He began to think very hard indeed.

To turn south would be fatal. He could never hope to climb the steep and bare slopes in time to reach some spot where he might make a stand. To turn north would also be madness. Then he would be the advancing point of a triangle with the two bands narrowing the angle till he would be caught in the deadly crossfire at close range. He turned his attention to the front.

Where he rode, the ground on either side was bare, but some distance ahead began a straggle of chaparral that flanked the trail on either side. Mostly the brush was too low to afford concealment for a horse and rider, but toward the center of the stretch was a patch of higher growth perhaps a hundred yards in extent. He studied the men racing down from the north and estimated they should hit the trail at a little beyond the growth. He formulated a desperate plan that might possibly work. At least it was better than nothing. He slowed Shadow's gait a bit, although he knew he was gambling against a lucky shot bringing him down. He had to take the chance, for it was necessary to the success of his well nigh hopeless stratagem that the two bands should arrive at the line of growth at approximately the same time.

Exultant shouts and a crackle of shots sounded as the pursuers behind closed the gap. Slade held Shadow in till the last possible second and again gave him his head. The men behind were dangerously close now and those from the north were sweeping down to be in on the kill.

The flying black reached the first fringe of growth and sped on, the scattered bushes flashing past in a misty blur. He reached the tall stand and in an instant was in the deeper shadow. Midway through the thicket, Slade jerked him to a sliding halt, whirled him and forced him into the brush on the left. He drew both guns and waited.

Scant seconds later he heard the drumming hoofs of the pursuit, swiftly loudening. Then he heard the clash of irons as the men from the north neared the trail. Another instant and they were upon it, with the band from the west pounding toward the stand of tall growth.

Slade waited a moment longer, then he opened fire with both guns. With the left he sent a stream of lead hissing toward the men from the west. His right-hand gun poured bullets at the band from the north that was just coming into view.

Yells, curses, howls of pain and a mad jangle of bit-irons and popping of saddle leather echoed the reports. Slade slammed his empty guns into their sheaths and sent Shadow surging north through the brush. Behind sounded a veritable pandemonium of bellowing men, cracking guns and snorting horses; the two bands had met head-on. Before the raging and utterly confused outlaws got untangled, Shadow was three hundred yards from the thicket and going like the wind over the broken ground.

Shots sounded, bullets whistled past, but horse and man were untouched and by the time the outlaws got their shattered nervous systems enough under control for accurate shooting, Slade was out of range. With both bands behind him, he had no fear of being overtaken. Glancing back he saw the two groups had merged and, realizing the futility of pursuit, were riding west. A couple appeared to have trouble staying in their hulls, and there was one horse that appeared to have a body draped over the saddle.

Pulling to a halt, Slade watched them grow small in the distance. Then he veered Shadow more to the east and rode on. He thought it best not to regain the trail. No telling who he might meet and he preferred not to play his luck too strong.

"We made it," he told Shadow as he swabbed at the blood that trickled down his bullet-gashed cheek. "Which was more than I hoped for at one time. It was touch and go, but we made it."

However Slade was not at all pleased with himself. He had underestimated Murray De Spain's devilish shrewdness and had been neatly outsmarted, escaping the trap laid for him more by luck than anything else, he felt. With commendable but unsatisfactory hindsight he now realized that a watch had been kept on him and when he rode out of town the fact was immediately reported to the outlaw chief. His stratagem of riding southeast did not fool De Spain in the least. De Spain had guessed correctly what he would do and had laid his plans accordingly. Yes, De Spain had taken the trick, and he had come within the width of a frog's hair of winning the game, the forfeit of which, so far as Slade was concerned, was death.

On only one point was Slade pleased with the night's near misadventure. He was now convinced beyond a shadow of doubt that De Spain was running his contraband into Mexico by way of the Santa Helena Canyon. How? Slade didn't know, but if it was humanly possible to do so he intended to find out.

FIVE

THE RIDE OVER THE ROUTE HE FOLLOWED was a long and hard one. The sun was well up the eastern slant of the sky when Slade finally reached Tule. Thoroughly worn out, he tumbled into bed as soon as he had taken care of Shadow's wants and was almost instantly asleep. He slept until dusk, arose, enjoyed a dip in the icy waters of the big trough and shaved. Then, ravenously hungry, he headed for the Root Hog and something to eat.

When he reached the saloon he found Sheriff Horton already there and putting away a surrounding. He glanced inquiringly at Slade's wounded cheek.

"Somebody scratch you?" he asked.

"Sort of," Slade admitted. He gave his order to a waiter and then acquainted the sheriff with the previous night's happenings.

"That cunning wind spider seems to be always a jump ahead of me," he concluded. "He's the sort that can read your mind around a corner. Smart as a treeful of owls. But just the same I figure maybe he made a slip when he tried to have me drygulched there by the river. I consider it proof positive that he does run the stuff by way of the canyon.

"But," he added thoughtfully, "I've a notion he's so sure nobody can figure how he does it, that he isn't much bothered over me seeing the boats enter the canyon. And there's where he may be making a bad mistake. Over-confidence has been the bane of more than one of his sort. Over-confidence frequently translates into carelessness."

"Well, if he does run the stuff by way of the canyon I figure he's got a flock of trained condor-vultures working for him," grunted the sheriff. "As I told you before, birds have been known to starve to death in that canyon, but maybe one of those big buzzards could make it out with a rifle or two."

"Your theory may not be so far-fetched at that," Slade smiled. "It does look like De Spain has something capable of climbing those trails with loads, which we're both agreed horses or mules could not."

"If he has a small army of peons working with him he might do it," the sheriff observed thoughtfully. "A man might be able to pack a rifle or two on his back and still climb the trails."

"Yes, but such a conclusion presupposes that Captain Ramirez and his *rurales* have suddenly gone blind. They are continually scouring the country to the south and so many men couldn't slip out of the villages without being noticed. Ramirez would get suspicious and he'd grab off a travelling gent or two and persuade them to do a little talking. And they have interesting ways of persuading a man to talk, down in Mexico. No, I'm afraid that's out. He's not using man power for transport from the river bed to the rimrock, but I still believe the stuff goes by way of the canyon."

"Maybe you're right," admitted the sheriff, "but I still think you're barking up the wrong tree."

He regarded his young table companion curiously for a moment. "Walt, how'd you come to tie up with the rangers in the first place?" he asked suddenly. "You're an educated man and could make a lot more in private life than the rangers are able to pay you."

"Well, it's a good deal of a story," Slade smiled.

"I'd like to hear it," said the sheriff.

"It was this way," Slade replied. "When I graduated from a college of engineering I had planned to take a post graduate course, specializing in certain phases of engineering, to round out my education. But things hadn't been going so good for us. You know how it was in the lower Panhandle a few years back—droughts in the summer, blizzards in the winter, and the cattle market in bad shape. The final result was that Dad lost his spread. It hit him hard, well nigh broke his heart to lose the old place. I firmly believe it's what killed him, for he died shortly afterward."

"Wouldn't be surprised," conceded the sheriff. "Hard on old folks to have to pull up stakes and start all over again."

Slade nodded and continued. "Well, that made the postgraduate course out of the question, and I hadn't tied onto a job as yet."

"Sort of at loose ends," commented the sheriff.

"That's so," Slade admitted. "So when Captain Jim McNelty, who was one of Dad's life-long friends, suggested that I join the rangers and continue my studies in spare time, I decided it was a good notion and took him up on it."

"But that was several years back," interpolated the sheriff.

"True," Slade agreed. "Quite a while ago I'd gotten from private study all and more than I could have hoped for from the postgrad, and I'm all set to enter my profession. But I'll have to admit that ranger work has sort of gotten a hold on me. It interested me when I worked some with Captain Jim during summer vacations, and my interest has increased. Perhaps I'm being foolish, but so far I haven't been able to bring myself to sever connections with the outfit. Oh, I will after a while, but I can't see as there's any great hurry. I'm young and there's plenty of time to become an engineer. Guess I'll stick with the rangers for a while yet."

"I can understand how you feel," nodded Horton. "Well, I've got to be getting back to the county seat, but I'll be down here again in a few days. Try and stay in one piece till I get back."

"I'll try," Slade promised, adding, "but I won't guarantee it with Murray De Spain mavericking around in the section."

After breakfast, Slade wandered around the town for a while. He replenished his stock of provisions and bought more cartridges. Then he retired to his room over the stalls to smoke and think. Some time after dark, he saddled up and again rode east and turned south. This time, however, he did not circle west but continued till he reached the Rio Grande below the south mouth of the canyon, no great distance from where the river, after flowing almost due north, again began its eastward trend toward the distant Gulf of Mexico.

The dawn was not far off and Slade was anxious to get across the river before the sun rose. He rode east for some distance until he discovered a trail that ran to the water's edge. It showed signs of being fairly well travelled and he reasoned that here there should be a ford that would provide a precarious crossing even in times of high water. He decided to take a chance and put Shadow to the water.

There was a ford, but the river, though it had fallen somewhat, was still dangerously high. They had to swim for it in the middle of the stream but they reached the far bank without mishap. Before the rising sun flooded the wild country with a sheen of gold they were well into the hills that flanked the canyon rim. Slade rode steadily, paralleling the gorge, until he had covered what he estimated to be half the canyon's extent. If the smugglers did transport by way of the Santa Helena he figured that they would do it from somewhere in the upper canyon, above the practically impassable rapids farther down. He sought out a favorable thicket and left Shadow in a little cleared space beside a trickle of water.

"Be seeing you, I hope," he told the black and started on his hazardous way to the canyon rim on foot.

Before the sun had crossed the zenith, Slade began to be of the opinion that Sheriff Horton knew what he was talking about when he insisted the game trails along the rim and down the walls could be negotiated only by lizards and mountain goats. The rock ledges were cracked and worn and slippery, with the water, dark and deep, swirling below. At times he was forced to clamber over rock slides or under great boulders, and even worm his way through narrow openings in the scatterings of talus. Progress was slow and the going exhausting in the extreme. Finally he gave it up for the day, worked back into the hills, where travel was easier, and returned to the thicket where he had left his horse. He was weary and footsore and rather discouraged.

It began to look as if his hunch was off-trail.

Small wonder the *rurales* didn't bother to patrol this section, he reflected gloomily as he surveyed the forbidding terrain rolling away from the canyon rim to the blue mountains in the distance. A crow would have to pack his rations with him across that or starve to death!

In the clearing by the brook he made a fire and cooked a meal of bacon, eggs, a dough cake fried in the bacon fat and a bucket of coffee. After eating he felt considerably better and somewhat more optimistic. There were still five or six miles more to explore before reaching the north mouth of the canyon. In the morning he'd ride on ahead to where he had left off and start again. He curled up beside the fire and went to sleep.

The following morning was well on and Slade estimated he was some three miles from the north mouth of the canyon when he at last got a break. He had been forced to detour an impossible stretch of the rim and was a considerable distance back in the hills when he came upon a faint track that showed signs of recent usage. It was scored by the marks of horses' irons and by narrower prints that could only have been left by mule hoofs. His eyes glowed with excitement. The condition of the prints told him that they had been made by a fairly large number of animals within the past few days.

Turning, he gazed toward the ominous rim

of the canyon. The trail apparently led toward it but he could see little because of the thick chaparral growth through which it ran. Eagerly he set out to follow the tracks. He was within five hundred yards of the rim when the trail branched, and here the tracks were scattered and numerous. The mules had undoubtedly been tied or held here. He examined the prints carefully to ascertain if the horses had taken one fork or the other. Suddenly he paused, staring at the ground.

"Now what in blazes!" he exclaimed aloud.

Amid the mule and horse tracks were other prints such as he had never seen before and which he was at a loss to catalogue. They were roughly round, with no frog marks, and small. Almost like somebody had tied a rag over a little mule's hoof, he reflected. He shook his head in bewilderment and gazed toward the rim aglow in the afternoon sunlight. Castles and spires seemed to tower along the canyon's path and over them crept deep, vivid tones of color in ever-changing harmony. Shaking his head again, he dropped his glance to the branch of the trail that swerved away from the track leading to the rim and was swallowed up by the chaparral. Scarring its surface were many of the strange prints that so excited his curiosity. He hesitated, then decided to follow the side fork. He had to find out what left such marks on the ground. Instinctively he moved forward with caution, pausing often to peer and listen.

As he progressed he became aware of a sound other than the low murmur of the rushing water in the canyon's depths—a strange bubbling and grunting, varied occasionally by thin bleats. The sounds loudened as he crept on.

In the eagerness aroused by his curiosity as to what might be the author of the unusual sounds, he quickened his step. He swerved around a bristle of growth and abruptly found himself on the edge of a small clearing completely surrounded by thicket. He did not at once observe other details—he had other things to think about. For standing not a dozen paces distant was a man with a rifle in his hands.

SIX

WITH A YELL OF SURPRISE and alarm the fellow clamped the rifle butt to his shoulder. His eyes glinted along the sights.

Slade hurled himself sideways and down in the split second before the black muzzle gushed flame and smoke. He heard the bullet screech over him, saw the rifle muzzle jerk down for a second shot, but before the man could pull trigger again, both Slade's guns let go with a rattling crash.

The man reeled back as if struck by a mighty fist. The rifle dropped from his hands. He spun around and fell headlong, his limbs jerking and twitching. Slade leaped to his feet, guns ready, but the rifleman was decidedly dead, or appeared to be.

Taking no chances, Slade strode forward, tense and alert. He turned the body over and gazed into a dark, contorted face.

"Another 'breed," he muttered.

Straightening up, he listened intently for a sound of approaching hoofbeats. He didn't pack any authority in Mexico and if a detachment of *rurales* patrolling the section had heard the shooting and decided to investigate, he might find himself in an unpleasant situation and have some embarrassing questions to answer. There would be nobody to back up his contention that he fired in self-defense.

But no sound broke the silence, for a moment. Then it was broken in a manner that caused Slade to jump and whirl around, a chorus of bleats and bubbling groans. He swept the clearing with his gaze and promptly forgot all about the *rurales* and everybody else.

Near the far side of the clearing was a small corral, and back of the bars were a score or so of extraordinary creatures.

They were sturdy little beasts something over three feet high at the shoulders and perhaps five feet in length. Their bodies were covered with long woolly hair nearly white in color. For tails they had mere stumps. Their necks were astonishingly long, surmounted by dog-like heads with perky ears and mild, questioning eyes. Their legs were also long and terminated in queer round two-toed hoofs.

For moments Slade stared in astonishment, utterly at a loss as to what the strange animals might be. Then remembrance rushed upon him. And the mystery of the apparently impossible canyon trails was solved!

"For the love of Pete!" he exploded. "South American llamas! The 'camels' of the Andes Mountains!"

There was no doubt about it, that was what the

critters were. The diminutive cousins of the desert camels of Africa and Asia, which the Peruvians used to carry loads over mountain trails where no other beasts of burden could go. But how in the jumping blue blazes did they come to be here in northern Mexico?

Abruptly he recalled that people said Murray De Spain had spent a couple of years in Peru, where not unlikely he became familiar with llamas and their uses. But again, how the devil did he manage to transport the animals to Mexico?

Then Slade remembered something else that up to the moment he had forgotten. Jefferson Davis, when Secretary of War, had brought camels from Africa to be used for transport on the deserts of Texas and Arizona, an experiment that failed. Even now it was said that a few descendants of the unwieldy "ships of the desert" roamed the Arizona badlands, scaring the devil out of horses and mules and causing prospectors and other desert rats to bring in tall tales of ghosts or devils they had seen or heard. Emulating Davis, the Mexican government had introduced llamas from the Andes into the mountain sections of the country. But the creatures, removed from their natural habitat, did not thrive and refused to breed. Eventually the few that survived were turned loose to fend for themselves, just as the Arizona camels had been. Apparently some had been able to adapt themselves to new conditions, and the canny De Spain had tied onto a number of them or their offspring. The little beggars could pack a hundred-pound load straight up a cliff. If there was anything like a trail down the canyon wall, negotiating it would be an easy task for the llamas.

Slade believed there was such a trail and intended to make sure. First, however, more immediate matters demanded attention. He carried the body into the brush, stuffed it in a crack between two rocks and covered it with leaves and twigs. He was engaged in this task when an inquiring snort caused him to turn quickly.

Peering at him from a clump of growth was an amiable-looking mule.

"Howdy!" he greeted the animal. "Reckon you belonged to this jigger. He won't be needing you anymore but I can use you to get back where I left my horse. And with you missing, too, who-ever comes looking for him will figure the scalawag just got tired of waiting and wandered off somewhere, or so I hope."

He rubbed the mule's nose and the docile creature obediently followed him to the clearing where it began contentedly cropping grass.

Slade thoroughly explored the clearing. There was a small spring inside the corral and ample forage for the llamas was scattered about. Further investigation revealed a brush lean-to built in the edge of the growth. Under it was a saddle and bridle and some tumbled blankets. Also a small store of provisions, enough to last about two days, Slade estimated. Which meant that the dead man had expected an early relief.

And which also meant, Slade reasoned, that very likely a convoy of contraband would be ready to take off for the south the following night. The llamas would bring the stuff up from the canyon floor and on the rimrock the mules would take over and transport it to the interior.

Slade next turned his attention to the fork of the trail that disappeared in the direction of the canyon rim.

As he expected, the track led straight over the rim. It was a hair raising path that wound along dizzy ledges dipping down the precipitous side of the gorge. It ended on a shelf a dozen yards in width that was some twenty feet above the canyon floor. A continuation beyond the shelf flowed down a last gentle slope to a little strip of beach flanking the water's edge. The beach was covered with scattered boulders and at either end was a jumble of rocks and stony spires. Here the river ran straight and continued to do so for nearly a mile. Gazing downstream between the encroaching walls Slade saw that only a few hundred yards beyond was a veritable maelstrom of rapids and wild water which foamed and spouted over jutting black fangs and swirled in whirlpools. In that watery waste no boat of the type used for transport by the smugglers could hope to live.

Yes, this was it, the spot where the boats tied up and their cargo was transferred to the backs of the llamas who carried it up the steep trail to the rimrock where sturdy mules waited to receive it. The scheme was almost foolproof.

Slade studied the immediate terrain. At either end of the stretch of beach was an ideal hole-up, from which the landing point would be commanded. He rolled a cigarette, leaned against a boulder and tried to decide the best way to take advantage of the situation. With a little teamwork on the part of Captain Ramirez and his *rurales*, it should be possible to bag the whole outfit at one swoop. And with luck, even De Spain himself. And after the trouble the former load got mixed in, Slade thought it quite possible that De Spain would be present to superintend the handling of the next one.

Pinching out his cigarette he toiled up the trail to the rimrock. Arriving at the clearing he saddled the mule and rode back to where he left Shadow. He got the rig off the mule and turned it loose. It immediately began cropping the rich grass and showed it was able to care for itself. Mounting Shadow he sent him north by west until he had circled the canyon.

The river had fallen greatly in the past few days and the crossing was easy to negotiate. Riding at a steady pace, Slade reached Tule a couple of hours after dark. He was elated to find Sheriff Horton in the little office he maintained at the mining town, talking with his deputies.

"Changed my mind about riding north," Horton explained. "Sort of developed a feeling you might need me and decided to stick around till you showed up."

"I'm mighty glad you did," Slade told him and proceeded to outline his discoveries. The sheriff swore in astonishment.

"And that's how they do it," he marvelled. "I've read about those critters and saw pictures of them. That infernal De Spain is a whizzer, all right. Think of him corralling those critters and putting them to use! There won't be any peace till that sidewinder stretches rope or is behind bars."

"I suppose you can contact Ramirez without trouble?" Slade asked.

"Sure, I can get hold of him tomorrow," the sheriff replied.

"That'll be fine," Slade said. "I figure there'll be a shipment coming through tomorrow night. Ramirez must be familiar with the country down there and should have no difficulty locating that trail. Tell him that when he faces north, the clearing is directly in line with El Solitario, the big mountain that straddles the county line. And on the canyon rim nearby is a tall chimney rock which resembles a church spire. The clearing is just about three miles below the canyon mouth."

"That should give him plenty to work on," nodded the sheriff. "I'll be with him and I'm pretty familiar with the country myself. I figure we won't have any trouble. What do you figure to do?"

"I plan to be down in the canyon," Slade replied. "With a little luck I should be able to hold the boat crew—not likely to be more than five or six altogether."

"You figure to tackle 'em alone?"

Slade nodded.

"That you won't!" Deputy Pete Crane, a spidery little man with a cast in one eye, announced cheerfully. "I'm going along. How about you fellers?" he asked, turning to his companions.

"Reckon we could do worse," laconic Clate Doran observed.

"I'd get lonesome here all by myself," added Tom Halsey.

"You'll be taking a chance," Slade warned, "and remember, we have no official authority down there and if something should go wrong we may find ourselves in trouble with the Mexican authorities."

"Guess we'll chance it," said Crane, beginning the manufacture of a cigarette.

"Okay, then," Slade nodded. "And I'm mighty glad to have you along. Horton, don't forget that Cavorca has spies everywhere and if they spot you palavering with Ramirez they may get suspicious and figure something's in the wind."

"They won't see me," the sheriff assured him. "I'll take care of that angle."

"Pete," Slade said to Crane, "do you think you could get hold of a boat that will carry the four of us? I think it would be better if we slide down the river and into the canyon that way, along about dark."

"Yep, I know a fishing jigger at Lolitos who'll let us have one. He's a right hombre and will keep his mouth shut. It's a good boat, one we can row up against the current if need be."

"That'll be fine," Slade said. "Doran, you go with Pete; leave here in the afternoon. Tom and I will follow later. That way we won't attract much attention if somebody is keeping a watch."

"And I'll ride south later tonight," said the sheriff. "I don't figure to have any trouble locating Ramirez, but if I do have trouble getting hold of him and you fellers get caught between the bunch in the boat and the others coming north with the mules, you'll find yourselves on a mighty hot spot."

"We'll have to risk it," Slade replied, "and I've a hunch everything is going to work out right."

“Hope so,” grunted the sheriff, “but that De Spain hellion is something to reckon with, and don’t you forget it.”

“I’m not underestimating him,” Slade answered. “I did that a couple of times and ended up coming out of the little end of the horn. He’s smart and he’s smooth, but I’ve a notion this time he’ll slip up. Well, I’m going to get some sleep; liable not to get much tomorrow night, or else a mighty long one.”

“Nice way to look at it,” snorted Horton. “That makes me feel real good. Be seeing you tomorrow night, I hope.”

SEVEN

A COUPLE OF HOURS AFTER SUNDOWN the following day found Slade and the three deputies afloat on the Rio Grande. The night was very dark, the moon being still below the horizon, the gloom leavened only by a faint glow of starlight and the phosphorescent gleams of the hurrying water.

"I figure they won't show up until around midnight or a little later," Slade told his companions. "Then the moon will be straight overhead and sending light into the canyon."

Less than a mile ahead yawned the black mouth of the Santa Helena, toward which the current swept the little boat at good speed. There was no need for the oars on the down trip.

The boat shot between the towering walls, the glow of the starlight vanished and the echoing gorge was pitch black.

"Have your oars ready," Slade cautioned. "I was mighty careful to estimate the distance as I rode up the river yesterday and I think I can pinpoint the stretch of beach, but if we run past it in the dark and get into the rapids below, well, De Spain and his bunch won't have us to worry about."

It was not pleasant, rushing along through the

black dark, like Charon ferrying souls across the Styx, Slade thought. The rush of the water echoing back from the rock walls was confusing and would drown the roar of the approaching rapids. Slade strained his eyes to pierce the gloom, tried to estimate correctly the speed at which the boat was travelling. He recalled that the canyon widened somewhat just above the beach and kept his gaze fixed on the ebon line of the rimrock far above.

"I think it's right ahead," he exclaimed suddenly. "Back water and veer to the right."

With his plainsman's uncanny sense of distance and direction, Slade had not been at fault. A little light filtered down from the star-strewn sky as the walls drew farther apart and a moment later he spotted the beach. They made the landing without difficulty and hauled the little boat ashore, concealing it behind boulders at the far end.

"Now all we can do is hole up and wait," Slade said. "Moon will be sending light down here before long."

"Maybe," observed Halsey. "Clouds in the sky tonight. Hope they don't thicken up."

"I don't believe they will," Slade predicted. "They're pretty well scattered and are travelling slowly. Not much wind up above, as would be the case if a real storm were approaching."

The little posse took up positions among the

rocks, keeping close together. Then came the most trying part of a ruckus, when nerves are strained by waiting and unpleasant and apprehensive reflections crowd into the mind.

The east rim of the canyon began to glow. A tiny line of silver flame appeared against the sky and the light increased as the moon climbed higher and higher until it was directly overhead and casting its beams straight into the gorge, causing the sands of the beach to glitter brightly. The river was a flood of molten silver, but under the chimney rocks where the four officers crouched was deep shadow. Directly above them was the broad bench from which the dizzy trail climbed to the rimrock.

The situation, for the moment, was ideal for the small posse, but complications were in order. Slade's weather prediction was proving somewhat inaccurate. High in the sky the wind was strengthening, the clouds hurrying before it. When one of these drifted across the face of the moon, the gorge was shrouded in deep gloom.

It was during one of these periods of darkness that the smugglers' boat arrived. Slade's keen ears detected a sound above the rush of the river.

"Get set," he whispered to his companions, "there's something moving out there."

Slowly the cloud which obscured the moon drifted on. It thinned to ragged streamers and the silvery light poured down, revealing the loaded boat moored to the bank. Beside it were half a dozen men who had just stepped ashore.

"Let's go!" whispered Slade. He stepped from the shadow, a gun in each hand; the deputies fanned out on either side of him. "Elevate!" he shouted. "You're covered! Up, I said!"

The astounded smugglers whirled to stare into unwavering gun muzzles. They mouthed and muttered but shot their hands into the air.

And a thick black cloud swept across the moon!

Slade dimly saw the outlaws scatter in every direction. He fired as fast as he could pull trigger. A yell of pain echoed the shots. Instantly the gorge was a-bellow with gunfire. Lead stormed about the posse.

"Behind the rocks!" Slade shouted, hurling himself in back of a boulder. The deputies, still shooting, followed his example. Red flashes continued to stab toward them from the dark. They could hear the outlaws scrambling over the boulders and fired at the sounds and the flashes, but it was blind work and a hit would be scored only by accident. A moment later the firing ceased.

Slowly the cloud drifted on. Once again the moonlight streamed down, at an angle, now, for the moon was working toward the far edge of the cliffs. Revealed was a body sprawled near the beached boat. Of the remaining outlaws nothing could be seen.

“Holed up behind those rocks at the other end,” Slade said. “Didn’t notice anybody who looked like De Spain, did you?”

“Nobody who looked like what you said he looked like,” Pete Crane replied. “Figure he wasn’t with them.”

“Then he’s with the bunch coming up from the south with the mules, I’ll bet a hatful of pesos on that,” Slade said. “I wish he was here. He’s too darned smart to have running around loose. He may figure a way to put it over on Ramirez.

“This is a mess,” he added. “They can’t get out, but neither can we. And if De Spain and his bunch get here first, we’re going to find ourselves on a hot spot.”

He raised himself a little for a better look. A gun banged at the far end of the beach and a slug fanned his face. The deputies returned the fire, chipping fragments from the boulders. Answering shots kept them huddled behind their own protection.

“Hold it!” Slade ordered. “We’re just wasting ammunition. Watch close for a hellion to show himself, then let him have it. This is getting too interesting for comfort.”

Slow minutes passed, and then abruptly on the bench above the beach birthed a reddish glow. Slade stared at it in astonishment as it swiftly strengthened.

Suddenly a man appeared at the lip of the bench, holding aloft a huge bundle of burning brush. The light glared on the face of Murray De Spain!

Slade's gun jutted forward, but before he could pull trigger De Spain had hurled the blazing bundle and ducked back out of sight.

The brush hit the canyon floor, flared up in leaping flame. Instantly the whole scene was bright as day.

From the bench sounded a roar of guns. Tom Halsey gave a hollow groan and sank down motionless. A second later Doran pitched from behind the boulder that only partially sheltered him and lay still.

"Two down and two to go," Pete Crane observed cheerfully as he fired at the bench. "Looks like curtains, feller."

"Maybe not," Slade answered between shots. "The fire's flickering out and the moon's behind the rimrock. Be dark in a minute."

At the far end of the beach the holed-up outlaws were yelling with triumph and peppering the boulders with bullets. One showered chips of stone into Slade's face. Crane cursed viciously as another grained the flesh of his arm.

"Keep down," Slade cautioned. "They can't see us from down there and we're in pretty good shape from the bunch on the bench. Maybe we can hold out."

"I doubt it," growled Crane, "but I sure hope I get a chance to take that yaller-haired hellion with me when I go."

As the darkness closed down the shooting ceased. Slade and the deputy lay motionless, listening intently and wondering what would come next.

Several minutes passed. Then again the ominous glow appeared on the bench. At the same instant Slade's ears caught a scuffling sound somewhere above.

"Look out," he told Crane. "I think they're getting ready to rush us. The bunch down among the rocks will join in. Here comes the flare!"

Again a bundle of burning brush spun through the air, but this time the man who hurled it kept back out of sight.

"Shoot at the lip of the bench," Slade told his companion. "Maybe we can hold them back."

"For a minute," Crane replied, once more cheerful. "See you on the other side, feller, and we'll talk it over."

Slade nodded grimly, of the opinion that Crane had the right of it; they had but minutes to live. He cocked his guns, crouched ready as the light flared brightly.

Suddenly from the bench sounded a crackling of shots, wild yells, howls of pain, curses, and a voice bellowing orders in Spanish.

Slade let out an exultant whoop. "Not this time,

Pete," he cried. "Ramirez and his boys have made it! They've caught the devils settin'."

From the bench boomed Sheriff Horton's voice, "You down there, Slade?"

"Right this way," Slade shouted back. "Take care of those hellions at the other end of the beach."

But the hellions at the other end of the beach did not wait to be "taken care of." Four men leaped to their feet, outlined by the blazing brush, their hands in the air, howling for mercy which the *rurales* appeared reluctant to grant. They were lining sights with them when Captain Ramirez shouted, "Hold it, we want prisoners!"

Down the path streamed the Mexican mounted police, nearly a score of them. In the front was Captain Jose Ramirez, a huge man with a fierce mustache. He held a cocked gun in each hand. Beside him was Sheriff Horton.

The four outlaws were quickly seized and securely bound. Slade strode forward.

"Did you get De Spain?" he asked eagerly.

"Blast it, no!" growled Horton. "He got away. Killed two men, went through us like a greased pig and up the trail in the dark. We were too darn busy to follow him."

"And no way to tell which way he'll turn when he reaches the rimrock," Slade said bitterly. "That devil always gets the breaks, or makes them, rather."

Captain Ramirez spoke up. "Perhaps we can obtain some information from the prisoners," he suggested. "They may know what your *amigo* De Spain has in mind."

"If you can get them to talk," Slade said.

"They'll talk," the *rurales* commander declared cheerfully. "Down here we have ways of making men talk. I will take them up the trail a ways and question them. No, no, *Capitan*, you had best remain where you are. I will handle this matter."

Slade didn't argue the point. He felt that if he didn't witness what took place in the darkness of the trail he would undoubtedly sleep better.

With four grim *rurales* herding them along, the prisoners ascended the trail with Captain Ramirez and vanished from sight. Some minutes of silence followed.

"Do you think he can get them to talk?" Sheriff Horton wondered dubiously.

At that instant from the darkness above came a squealing cry that rose and fell for several seconds and then abruptly stilled. Slade felt his scalp prickle, the palms of his hands grow clammy with cold sweat.

"Yes, I think he can," he belatedly answered the sheriff's question.

After another period of silence, Captain Ramirez reappeared, grinning like a cheerful demon. "They talked," he announced laconically. "I took one aside and reasoned with him, gently.

Soon he became quite voluble. To make sure there would be no mistake, I took a second apart and spoke with him. The two stories agreed in detail. It would seem that Señor De Spain planned to travel west tomorrow, to Arizona. His object to establish a base somewhere near the town where silver is mined, Tombstone, I believe it is called, from which he will smuggle arms into Sonora, where there are also many rebels who serve the unspeakable Sebastian Cavorca. I gather that there are many outlaws in and near that town and that they are strongly entrenched. Doubtless De Spain will enlist their aid."

"Sounds reasonable," Slade conceded. "Well, anyhow I know where to look for him, thanks to you, Captain."

"Rather I should thank you for the opportunity you gave me to smash this band of *ladrones*," returned the captain. "*Gracias*, *Capitan*, *gracias*!"

"You going after De Spain?" Sheriff Horton asked curiously.

"Of course," Slade replied. "He's responsible for the death of two Texas citizens, even though the killing occurred on Mexican soil."

"You won't have any official authority in Arizona," warned the sheriff.

"Perhaps not," Slade admitted, "but this business has become a personal matter between De Spain and myself. Clate Doran and Tom Halsey came here with me of their own free will, to lend me a hand. I feel responsible for what happened and I don't propose to let De Spain get away with it and go unpunished."

Sheriff Horton nodded his understanding. "Good hunting," he said briefly.

"We might as well load the bodies of Halsey and Doran into the boat and take them back with us for decent burial," Slade said. "*Adios*, Captain, I hope to see you again."

On the way up the river Sheriff Horton told of what happened on the rimrock.

"We grabbed a couple up there who had been left to guard the mules and the llamas," he explained. "Of course, when the rest of the hellions who were making their way down the trail heard the shooting in the canyon they hightailed down to find out what was going on. We heard the shooting, too, and didn't waste any time scooting after them."

"Lucky for Pete and me that you didn't," Slade said. "It was beginning to look like we were due for the last roundup. Well, Captain Ramirez intercepted a hefty shipment of arms and ammunition and just about busted up De Spain's bunch in this section, so I guess something was accomplished. But at the cost of several lives," he added bitterly.

Looking at his bleak face and icy eyes, Sheriff Horton was confident that there would be a day of reckoning for Murray De Spain.

EIGHT

TWO DAYS LATER SLADE RODE west by north. He had thought of making straight for the railroad and taking a train to Arizona, but after prolonged reflection had decided otherwise. He'd tried that procedure once with Murray De Spain, and it didn't work. The two captured smugglers might have been right in their contention that De Spain was headed for Arizona, but then again they could have been wrong. De Spain might have some other destination in mind. Slade decided that his best bet was to follow the Border and try to pick up additional information on the way.

He completed the long ride to El Paso without misadventure. Here he paused for two days to afford Shadow an opportunity for a good rest, but on the morning of the third day he sat his tall horse and gazed west and north to the mountains of New Mexico.

"Horse," he said, "we don't pack any authority over there—yet, but we'll see, we'll see."

He rode on, following the old, old trail that for centuries was the trade route east and west. He rode steadily until he reached a little railroad station that had a telegraph office. Dismounting, he entered the office and approached the operator, who looked up inquiringly and a little apprehensively as the tall figure of El Halcon drew near.

"I'd like to send a message," Slade told him.

The operator frowned. "Listen, cowboy, this is a railroad telegraph office," he said in a surly voice. "No private messages go over this wire."

Slade slipped something from a cunningly concealed secret pocket in his broad leather belt and laid it on the table between them. The operator stared at the famous silver star set on a silver circle, the universally honored and respected badge of the Texas Rangers, and abated his tone.

"Well, I reckon that's different," he said. "Let's have it."

Slade quickly wrote out a message.

> Am in New Mexico. Expect to be in Arizona. It started in Texas.
>
> W. J. Slade

The message was addressed to Captain James McNelty, Texas Ranger Post Headquarters.

"You should receive an answer in an hour or two, if Captain Jim isn't out sashaying around somewhere," Slade said as the operator opened his key.

The answer came in a little less than an hour. It was terse and cryptic.

Know the governor of New Mexico.
Know the governor of Arizona, too.
See you when you get back to Texas.
McNelty

"I suppose the rules of your company forbid you to divulge the contents of messages sent or received?" Slade remarked suggestively to the operator as he stowed the message away.

"They do," replied the operator, adding emphatically, "and what you took out of that belt pocket says so more'n the rules do."

Slade chuckled and left the office. He chuckled again as he mounted Shadow and rode on.

"Foxy old jigger!" he remarked to Shadow, apropos of Captain Jim. "Know the governor of New Mexico! Know the governor of Arizona! Horse, I reckon we'll be able to pick up a little authority if we happen to need it.

"But," he added thoughtfully, "I'm afraid there's only one kind of 'authority' that will pack any weight with Murray De Spain."

His right hand automatically caressed the black butt of the big Colt sagging against his thigh.

Slade spent the night at a lonely ranchhouse set back some way from the trail.

"A big feller with yellow hair?" his host replied to a question. "Uh-huh, a feller answering that description went by here three days back. Didn't spend the night, just stopped for a bite to eat. Was riding just about the finest looking bay horse I ever laid eyes on. Almost up to the critter you fork. Friend of yours?"

"I'm very anxious to catch up with him," Slade equivocated.

The rancher didn't ask any questions, but the following morning when Slade rode away he remarked to his range boss, "If that big jigger was hankering to catch up with me, I wouldn't even stop when I got to the Pacific Ocean; I'd keep right on ridin' to China!"

Slade rode on in an exultant frame of mind. He was on Murray De Spain's trail, no doubt about that, and now he believed that the smugglers had been right, De Spain was headed for Arizona and doubtless Tombstone and Cochise County, notorious for one of the best organized, shrewdest and most powerful outlaw bands the Southwest ever knew.

At Lordsburgh, he again laid over a couple of days for Shadow's benefit. He knew there was scant chance of overtaking De Spain on the road unless he happened to suffer an accident. This was improbable—De Spain was not the sort liable to accidents.

Crossing the Arizona State Line near Cochise Head, he rode steadily until he reached Benson, where he turned sharply south on the Benson

Road. Tombstone, his destination of the moment, was less than thirty miles distant.

When Walt Slade rode into Tombstone on a day of blue skies and golden sunshine, the Silver City was at the height of its prosperity. There was no hint of the disaster, the most amazing in the annals of American mining, that it was soon to suffer and which would almost overnight change a roaring boom town into a sleepy village. The Contention, the Tough Nut, the Lucky Cuss, the Sulphuret and a score of other productive mines were pouring forth their seemingly inexhaustible treasure of precious metal. Tombstone, a mining town in the heart of cattle country, was not only a booming silver town but a cowboy capital as well. Tombstone had, so legend said, a dead man for breakfast every morning. It also had churches, schools, social clubs, lurid melodrama and refined culture. Inside the church the minister preached a sermon; outside, desperados shot up the street. The sheriff chased rustlers in one part of Cochise county while road agents robbed the stage only a few miles away. Ladies sat primly at pink teas while the whir of spinning roulette wheels, the slither of cards, the chink of bottle necks on glass rims and at times the boom of holster artillery, roared practically next door. Tombstone was the strangest pattern of contradictions the West ever knew or ever will know.

The cowhands who rode in from the San Pedro, the San Simon and other nearby valleys were not noted for refinement and gentle dispositions. The gentlemen who picked and shoveled and blasted in the mines were somewhat lacking in cultural attributes and peaceful inclinations. The two factions mixed in about the same manner as nitric acid and glycerine. The result, dynamite! And the gamblers, outlaws, plain desperados and ladies added the necessary sulphuric ingredient to achieve the ideal explosive. Tombstone took them all in its stride; pink teas and dance halls were both flourishing institutions.

Early frontier-town drink emporiums usually consisted of a plank laid across a couple of barrels and housed in a pole-and-sod leanto or a canvas tent. Tombstone saloons were somewhat different. The great mirror-blazing back bars were pyramided with glittering glassware and bottles of every shape and color. Gentlemen in ties and white coats presided at the "mahogany", and mahogany was no mere figure of speech. It was solid wood polished till it gleamed and reflected. Patrons sipped intricate cocktails cheek-by-jowl with others who downed slugs of straight whiskey without chasers. A sober business suit rubbed elbows with a blue flannel shirt, and neither resented the other. When a gentleman began remonstrating an acquaintance with a six-shooter and said acquaintance explained with another, the proceedings became lively. Peace was generally restored by a bartender or lookout with a persuasive sawed-off shotgun. The bars with their expensive mirrors and fittings were placed in the back of the room, farthest from the street, because exuberant individuals on the sidewalks sometimes practiced marksmanship on the plate glass windows. It was all good clean fun, but mirrors and imported vintages cost money and it's hard to collect from a corpse for damage done.

Tombstone's hectic activity never stilled for a minute. When a saloon, dance hall or gambling place opened, the keys were thrown away. They would not be needed, for the doors were never closed. The blaze of the noonday sun and the bonfire stars of Arizona were one and the same to Tombstone. Its growling rumble was as continuous as the thunder of the stamp mills at Charleston and Contention grinding out the silver that was Tombstone's life blood.

Tombstone's principal thoroughfare was Allen Street, paralleled by Tough Nut and Freeman. All three were business centers. Allen was wide, lined with business houses from the O.K. corral at one end to the Bird Cage Opera House, bawdy and notorious, at the other. Wall Street, New York, ends at a graveyard. Allen Street also ended at a place of death, for it was in the O.K. corral that the famous gunfight between the Earp faction and members of Curly Bill Brocius' gang occurred.

At the northwest corner of Allen and Fifth was the Crystal Palace, one of the most luxurious and famous of Tombstone's many saloons and gambling houses. Across from the Crystal Palace, on the northeast corner of Allen and Fifth, was the equally famous and even more luxurious Oriental Bar in which Wyatt Earp owned an interest. Wyatt, his brother Virgil, and gaunt, consumptive Doc Holliday, the Earps' trigger-man could usually be found there, with Buckskin Frank Leslie, one of the West's deadliest gun-slingers, presiding as head bartender and looking genial and harmless in his white garb.

Slade located suitable quarters for Shadow, and a room for himself in a small hotel nearby. Then, after freshening up a bit, he sauntered out to give the town a once-over.

It was not the first time he had visited Tomb-stone and he was not altogether unfamiliar with the Silver City. He lounged along Allen Street, inspecting places of interest, marvelling at the growth of the town in a short year. Everywhere was bustle and activity, prosperity and optimism. There was no hint of the doom that lay quiescent in the unplumbed depths of the dark and rugged hills to whose wealth of silver the town owed its being.

During the course of his stroll, Slade saw no

familiar faces. Only once was he accorded more than a casual glance by the busy townsfolk or the visiting cowhands, prospectors and others. It was when an old Mexican abruptly halted, removed his ragged sombrero and bowed low.

Slade returned his respectful greeting with a nod and a friendly smile and passed on. The Mexican gazed after him as one who sees a vision.

Toward evening, Slade made his way back along Allen Street and entered the Oriental Bar. The hour was still early and there was only a sprinkling of people in the big room. As he ordered a drink he was conscious of the concentrated gaze of three men standing at the far end of the bar. Their interest he felt sure was greater than that usually accorded a stranger in the Oriental.

One of the trio was a man approaching middle age. His bearing was soldierly, he had big features and a rather kindly expression. Beside him stood a cadaverous individual, thin to emaciation. There was a hectic flush on each prominent cheekbone, his countenance was saturnine and his eyes had a feverish glow. He was impeccably garbed in gray, the set of his perfectly fitting coat somewhat marred by the sawed-off shotgun strapped under his left arm.

The third, who Slade rightly guessed was brother to the older man, was tall and sinewy. He was blonde, wore a tawny drooping mustache and had the keenest and coldest pale eyes Slade had ever seen. He was young, about his own age, or perhaps a year or two older, anyhow approaching thirty, Slade decided, although the granite lines of his face made him appear older.

Slade did not need to be told that he was the famous frontier marshal of Wichita, Ellsworth and roaring Dodge City, now a Deputy United States Marshal, *Wyatt Berry Stapp Earp.*

NINE

AS SLADE SIPPED HIS DRINK, Wyatt Earp suddenly disengaged himself from the group and strolled forward. The slow, slithery movements of his gaunt, heavy-boned, loose-limbed and powerful frame suggested those of a lion. His hair was yellow as a lion's mane and when he spoke his deep voice was a lion-like growl.

"Howdy," he said.

"Howdy," Slade replied, without turning from the bar.

"Slade's the name, isn't it?" Wyatt Earp stated rather than asked.

"Right."

"Sometimes pack another name, something like—El Halcon?"

"Right."

Wyatt Earp's eyes opened a little, he hesitated an instant. "Just ride in?"

"Right."

"Don't you think it would be a good idea to keep on riding?"

"Wrong!"

Wyatt Earp's eyes widened a little more. He seemed at a loss how to proceed.

Slade set his empty glass on the bar and turned to face the marshal. Wyatt Earp was a stalwart six-footer but he had to raise his eyes a little to meet Slade's level gray gaze.

"Earp," Slade said, his voice soft and musical, "if you're speaking as a peace officer you're talking out of turn, and you know it. When you have something on me that makes it imperative for me to ride, you can act accordingly, as a peace officer. Otherwise, as a peace officer, lay off! If you're making a personal issue of the matter, well—" The pale, cold eyes and the black-lashed gray eyes locked and held.

Wyatt Earp understood perfectly the implication of that unfinished sentence. He slowly shook his tawny head. "No, I'm not making it a personal issue," he said. "I'm a peace officer and I shoot with no man unless I have to. As a peace officer I admit I have nothing on you—seems nobody is ever able to get anything on you, or so I've been informed. Heard you were headed this way, and we've got enough trouble here as it is. Perhaps I did speak out of turn. It's a free country and I reckon you got a right to be anywhere you wish so long as you don't abuse that right. No offense meant."

"None taken," Slade answered. "Have a drink."

"Don't mind if I do," said Wyatt Earp.

The silent Frank Leslie filled the glasses. Wyatt Earp drained his in a single swallow.

"One on the house," he said, jerking his head toward Slade. With a nod he walked back to join his brother Virgil, Town Marshal of Tombstone, and consumptive Doc Holliday, the coldest killer in Tombstone, and the fighting ace of the Earp faction.

As Buckskin Frank Leslie waited for Slade to empty his glass, his eyes met El Halcon's and he smiled faintly, which was a high compliment coming from that gentlemanly and utterly fearless scoundrel.

Slade finished his drink and walked out, with a nod to the silent group at the end of the bar.

"Well?" said Doc Holliday.

Wyatt Earp gazed after Slade. "There goes the most dangerous man that ever rode into Tombstone," he said. He recounted his conversation with Slade.

Doc Holliday gazed at him curiously. "And suppose you'd told him you were making a personal issue of it?" he asked.

"In my opinion," said Wyatt Earp, "I would have died."

Holliday stared at him incredulously. "You don't mean that, Wyatt?"

"Yes, I mean it," Wyatt Earp replied. "Gentlemen, you have just seen what happens once in a lifetime, a gunfighter without a flaw. Perfect coordination of hand and eye, with a clear, cold, hair-trigger brain to direct them and tell them what to do. That feller who told us the smartest and most dangerous outlaw in Texas, one that never gets caught, was headed this way, didn't exaggerate."

"Somehow I didn't cotton to that feller," Virgil Earp observed. "A fine-looking feller, all right, spoke well and talked like an educated man, but somehow I didn't take to him. And I'm still trying to figure how Slade got into the conversation. All of a sudden we were all talking about El Halcon and the fact that he 'peared to be heading for Arizona, as if we'd always known him, and we hadn't heard of him an hour before. Somehow that feller managed to slip him in without seeming to do so. Never said a thing against him except that folks back there figure him for an owlhoot too smart to get caught. But all of a sudden we were bothered about him and wondering when he'd show up. Feller sure did describe him to a T; I recognized him the minute he walked in the door."

"That feller never did make it clear just what *he* was doing here, did he?" remarked Doc Holliday.

"He didn't come right out and say, but I sort of gathered that he was interested in buying a cow ranch if he could find one for sale," Wyatt Earp said. "He asked a lot of questions about the San Pedro Valley and the San Simon Valley and the Animas Valley. Wanted to know if we were bothered much by rustlers and if the Mexicans raided across the Line and if there was a local market here for cattle. Seemed mighty interested in all the country down to the south of here. Reckon he's after a spread, all right. Maybe he'll tie onto one."

"Funny sort of name he had," commented Holliday. "De Spain—Murray De Spain."

"And somehow, I seem to have heard that name somewhere," Wyatt Earp remarked reflectively, "but for the life of me I can't recall when or where."

"Getting back to Slade," said Holliday, "what do you suppose he's doing here? Figure he might be going to join up with the Brocius bunch?"

"Could be," conceded Wyatt Earp, "only he gave me the impression of being more the lone wolf type. Of course, if he is the outlaw they say he is, he might figure on some good pickings in this section, just as a lot of other hellions have."

Wise old Virgil Earp put in a word. "In my opinion," he said, "he's here looking for somebody."

"You might have something there," agreed Holliday. "But who? Curly Bill Brocius himself? Joe Hill? John Ringo?"

"Possibly," said Virgil, "though I rather doubt it. I don't recall that any of those jiggers ever operated in Texas. Ringo was from Texas originally, I believe, but that was years ago, and Slade's young."

"They start their blood feuds young in Texas," Holliday grunted. "Say, I just happened to think of something. Maybe Johnny Behan brought him in."

The others stared at him. Then Wyatt shook his head. "Not likely, I'd say," he differed. "Sheriff Behan is our enemy, but I can't see him hiring a quick-draw man to do his fighting. Not Johnny's style. He works subtly, which makes him the more dangerous. But it's something to think about. You could be right. Be that as it may, I have a mighty strong feeling that that big ice-eyed devil showing up here means trouble."

Slade ate his dinner in a small and quiet restaurant on Second Street, where he could smoke and think without distraction. Summing up, he was pretty well pleased with his experience in the Oriental Bar. The peace officers in the persons of Wyatt and Virgil Earp appeared somewhat suspicious of him and his intentions. Which he felt would redound to his advantage. The word would get around and eventually to the ears of the powerful outlaw organization of Cochise County. He would be looked on by them, if not as an ally, at least one whose views were in accord with theirs. And it was from the fraternity opposed to law and order that he expected to gain information as to Murray De Spain's plans and movements.

That Curly Bill Brocius and his associates would quickly learn of De Spain's presence in the section was incontrovertible. Also it was quite likely that they would regard him askance as a potential rival for the control of their domain. Slade himself did not believe that De Spain had any intention to enter into competition with Curly Bill and his cohorts, who represented a murderous criminal organization that was the boldest and most powerful in the history of the Southwest. It would not be to De Spain's interest to do so, even though he might quickly build up an outfit of his own that would, if De Spain desired, pose a real threat to Brocius' outlaw empire.

It was evident that De Spain had arrived in Arizona alone, but south of the Border there were those awaiting his coming who would rally to him as the emissary of Sebastian Cavorca and who would be ready and willing to take part in any act of lawlessness he might suggest.

Slade knew that if he were to smash De Spain, he must do so before De Spain really got organized. Slade was convinced that the prisoners had been right when they told Captain Ramirez that De Spain planned to smuggle arms to the rebels in Sonora. This very likely meant that arrangements had already been made and De Spain would find assistants ready to hand when he put in an appearance. Even now he might be busily welding a force together. Slade believed he was.

Yes, without doubt De Spain's primary objective was to run rifles and ammunition across the Border, but Slade was familiar enough with the crafty outlaw's procedures to be confident that he would not be able to resist plucking a plump pear if opportunity presented—and there were plenty of opportunities in Cochise County. Slade predicted that the peace officers of the section were in for a lively time and some novel experiences. De Spain was ingenious in his methods and didn't run true to form. He was not the run-of-mine variety of brush popping owlhoot with a one-track mind and little imagination. Slade felt pretty sure that he'd soon pull something that would raise the hair on the heads of Wyatt Earp, Sheriff Behan and lots of others.

So far as he personally was concerned, De Spain would never forget what happened in Santa Helena Canyon, and he would be out to even up the score. And although it meant deadly danger for Slade, it might prove to be De Spain's "Achilles' heel." A man who seethes with hate and a desire for vengeance sometimes goes against his own better judgment, loses his sense of proportion and commits fatuous acts.

Slade wondered mildly how Wyatt Earp learned his identity, but he did not consider the problem a very obscure one. El Halcon was pretty well known in Texas and Tombstone was a focal point for restless spirits from all over the Southwest. Somebody from Texas had recognized him, just as the old Mexican on Allen Street did, and had relayed the information to Wyatt. That was all.

Walt Slade didn't know it, but Murray De Spain had already gained a point. With uncanny perspicacity he had deduced that El Halcon would follow on his trail and had immediately taken steps to eliminate him in one way or another, to which events of the near future would add further proof.

TEN

ORDERING A LAST CUP OF COFFEE which he drank in leisurely fashion, Slade left the restaurant and strolled about the town some more. Finally he entered the Crystal Palace Saloon across the street from the Oriental Bar. As the Oriental was the stronghold of the Earp faction, so the Crystal Palace was the principal hangout for members of the Brocius gang when they visited Tombstone.

Slade found a place at the bar near a group of four men who stood somewhat apart. And once again he felt himself the cynosure of a battery of eyes. One of the nearby quartette was a bronzed, blue-eyed giant with dark kinky hair and snapping black eyes. Next to him was a bulky fat-faced person with a shifty gaze. The third was a lean sinewy individual of a saturnine cast of countenance. The fourth was a tall, broad-shouldered, well-formed and exceedingly handsome man with fine eyes and straight features that now wore a scowl.

Slade had never seen any of them before. He didn't know it, but they were Curly Bill Brocius, Ike Clanton, Joe Hill and John Ringo, Curly Bill's chief lieutenant, said by many to be the real brains of the Brocius gang.

Ringo, an educated man, splendidly brave, who had thrown his life away and was constantly tortured by regrets, was usually amiable and soft-spoken, but at a certain stage of drunkenness grew sullen, vicious and quarrelsome, and deadly. Ringo had at the moment arrived at that stage.

"It's him, all right," Curly Bill muttered in an undertone.

"Yes, it's him," Ringo said. The scowl on his face deepened. Abruptly he strode forward to where Slade stood, halting within arm's reach, and looked him up and down. And when he spoke, the tone of his voice was deliberately insulting.

"Man from Texas, aren't you?"

"Right," Slade replied composedly.

Ringo's voice took on an even more sneering note. "Well," he said, "I never knew of anything that was any good coming out of Texas."

Slade hit him, dispassionately, but with his two hundred pounds of bone and muscle back of his fist. Ringo's long body flew through the air and crashed to the floor, and stayed there.

With a yell of anger, Curly Bill grabbed for his gun. Then he froze, his whitening fingers gripping the butt of the Colt. He was looking into two unwavering black muzzles. His companions stood motionless, in strained, awkward positions.

Slade spoke, his voice soft and deadly, "If you

aim to take cards in the game, step up. I've got a trump for every trick you can play. Step up, boys, don't be bashful!"

But those experienced outlaws knew eyes and they knew hands. And each man of the trio felt that he was singled out for special attention. They hated to give back, but—

It was John Ringo who snapped the tension. He got to his feet heavily, rubbing his already swelling jaw, and he appeared cold sober. "Hold it, boys," he said. "No sense in starting a general row. I asked for it and I got it."

He turned to Slade. "My apologies," he said. "I was born in Texas."

Slade holstered his guns with the same effortless ease with which he had drawn them. He smiled, the flashing white smile of El Halcon that women, and men, found irresistible.

"Then I'd say," he observed, his voice all music, "that some rather fine things do come out of Texas."

"You have a right to your opinion, of course," Ringo answered in a tired voice, "but in this particular instance I fear you're wrong."

Before Slade could reply, a fussy little man wearing a ferocious scowl came bustling across the room. "Here! Here!" he exclaimed. "What's going on here? I'll have no gun-slinging."

"Oh, shut up, Johnny, and lay off," Ringo said wearily. "You're always behind the tailgate."

Sheriff John Behan gulped and goggled, but he didn't answer Ringo.

Though he would shoot a man as quickly as he would look at him, Curly Bill couldn't stay angry with anything or anyone for more than a few minutes. Now he bellowed with laughter.

"Belly up, everybody!" he shouted. "Drinks, bartender!" He grinned at Slade. "Come on, feller," he said, "you're with us!"

Wyatt Earp heard about the ruckus a short time after it occurred, from his younger brother Morgan, who happened to be in the Crystal Palace at the time.

"If it was a put-on act, it was a good one and played for keeps," Morgan declared. "John Ringo's got a knot on his jaw the size of my fist. But right now they're all thick as ticks on a sheep's back, with Johnny Behan hovering around 'em like a dog that isn't sure of his welcome."

Wyatt Earp swore in weary disgust. "See?" he said to Virgil. "Remember what I told you this afternoon? Trouble and more trouble! I've a notion to pull out for California. This blasted town's getting plumb ruined."

In the Crystal Palace, Curly Bill conversed jovially with Slade. "Heard you were headed this way," he suddenly said. "Heard you aimed to sort of take over hereabouts."

"Then you heard wrong," Slade told him. "I attend to my own business and don't interfere with anybody else's. I'm by myself and intend to stay that way."

"That's the ticket!" applauded Curly Bill. "Sometimes wish I'd always gone it alone myself. Got a notion I'd be better off if I had."

"I believe you would," Slade said, and meant it. He felt that if Bill Brocius had remained by himself, and honest, he would have made an outstanding success of life. He had all the earmarks.

A little later, Curly Bill decided to call it a night. "Got to be getting back to Galeyville, the other side of the Chiricahuas," he told Slade. "Drop in on me if you're over that way. You can usually find me around Nick Babcock's saloon. Spend most of my time there. Fun and raising the dickens for a week. And sick as a dog for a week afterwards. They sure sell rot gut licker in that pueblo. A heck of a life! You look like you don't drink much."

"I don't," Slade admitted.

"You're better off. Well, so long! Be seeing you."

As they rode out of town, Curly Bill remarked to his companions, "That Slade 'pears to be a regular feller. I've a notion that jigger who was telling us about him when he stopped at Galeyville had him all wrong. But he's a cold proposition, gents, a cold proposition!"

“And something more,” said John Ringo.

“What?”

A tortured look shadowed Ringo’s fine eyes. “What I always wanted to be and never was—a man!”

ELEVEN

AFTER A GOOD NIGHT'S REST, Slade also saddled up and rode out of town. He rode south by way of the Bisbee road for he wanted a look at the wild country around the Mexican Border. Somewhere down there Murray De Spain would choose a route for his smuggling trains. Perhaps he would run them by way of the San Simon Valley in Arizona and Skeleton Canyon winding through the wildest part of the Peloncillo Mountains to the Animas Valley in New Mexico, and across the Line into Mexico. Slade knew that route had long been favored by smugglers to and from Mexico. In Skeleton Canyon, Curly Bill Brocius and his bunch had ambushed a smuggler train, slain all but one of the Mexican guards and escaped with the Mexican silver—something like seventy-five thousand dollars worth. Bloodstained treasure that was squandered over the Galeyville bars during weeks of riotous living.

As Slade rode, his gaze roamed over a magnificent panorama of mountains and valleys. To the east towered the main range of the Chiricahuas, to the southwest the Huachucas, with the Santa Rita range almost due west in the farther distance. To the north loomed the

Dragoons, dark, rugged, sinister, where Geronimo had his stronghold from which he conducted his murderous raids, relentlessly harrying the thinly-settled land with a warfare of ambuscade and assassination.

It was wild, bleak country, but beautiful. Beautiful with the unspoiled majesty of the wastelands. But, like the arid hills that poured forth their treasure of silver once they were scratched by a miner's pick, a land of unlimited possibilities, with a past of tragedy, a bloody present and a mighty future.

Slade knew perfectly well that his departure would be noticed, and that quite likely the news would be quickly relayed to Wyatt Earp and Sheriff Behan.

Well, he didn't pay that much mind. If they wanted to have him followed, well and good. He had nothing to conceal, and if he desired to lose the tail he could quickly shake off any pursuit.

He couldn't say whether others were keeping tabs on him. He had undoubtedly been rather widely recognized as El Halcon from Texas, and it was not beyond the realm of possibility that Murray De Spain, if he was somewhere in the locality, as Slade firmly believed he was, would already have learned of his presence. That chance, however, he had to take.

In fact his departure from Tombstone was noted by others than friends of the peace officers.

And he was followed, by a lean little man dark of feature who was no slouch at trailing. He did not stick to the Bisbee road but kept in the hills, and he never let El Halcon out of his sight. When he was about twenty-five miles from Tombstone, Slade turned sharply south on a rutted trail, the unseen follower pulled up, then rode at a swift pace south, following a shortcut that would take him to the only settlement to which the road led, Naco on the International boundary separating Naco, Arizona from Naco, Sonora.

The trail which Slade followed, veering but little from its southward trend, soon ran through desert country with, in the far distance to the south, the white-tipped blue mountains of Mexico. For nearly ten miles Slade rode across the arid desolation and not until sunset did he reach the village. He continued until he was riding the wide, dusty street of Naco, Sonora, just across the Line. Naco had two streets, in fact, both dusty, both lined with one-story adobes. Scantily-dressed brown children peeked out through doorways or paused at their play in the grassless clay yards to stare at the horseman. A pretty *señorita* walking along the road had a sideways glance of bright eyes for him, while a *vaquero*, his saddle and bridle shining with silver conchas, gave him a friendly grin. Slade answered the attentions of all three with his flashing smile and a nod.

"Well, Shadow, once again we're where we don't rate a mite of authority except what I'm packing in leather," he told the horse. "Well, maybe we'll make out. First off is a surrounding of proper fodder for you."

Not far from the bull ring at the edge of the town, a large round arena enclosed by a wall, he found a small stable where Shadow could secure accommodations.

"I'll be back for him after a bit, but I want him to put on the nosebag and rest while I get something to eat myself," he told the smiling stablekeeper.

"He will be cared for, and be waiting when you return," the other assured him. "La Estralita, which you passed just before reaching my *meson*, has excellent food. The *cantinas* farther along the street sell fine beer, mescal and tequila. Farthest of all is El Tecolote—The Owl, where most men who ride from the north drink and dance."

He paused, gave Slade a swift, appraising glance. "But hard men gather there, Capitan, and a stranger does well to, as you would say, keep the skin from over the eyes."

"*Gracias*," Slade chuckled in appreciation of the friendly warning, "if I go there I'll try and keep them open."

The Mexican chuckled in turn. "And I doubt not that you will succeed."

At La Estralita, Slade enjoyed a hotly seasoned

meal washed down with really good wine. The service was leisurely and it was plain that a diner was expected to linger over his meal, which Slade did. He asked for coffee to finish his repast and was served some that wanted for nothing. After smoking a couple of cigarettes he strolled along the street, dropping into several of the *cantinas*, finding them lively, gay and friendly, but noting nothing of particular interest. He decided that the place the stablekeeper called the Owl would be his best bet, but before visiting that dubious rendezvous he returned to the stable and got his horse.

He located the place without difficulty, the name being painted in both Spanish and English across the dirty window. Nearby was a hitchrack at which stood several horses. He looped the split reins and tossed them over an empty peg. Shadow would remain right where he was and anybody who tried to put a hand on him would very likely lose half his arm. These matters attended to, he entered the *cantina.*

Very quickly Slade was of the opinion that when the stablekeeper said hard men foregathered in The Owl he wasn't talking through his hat. The fairly large crowd was made up of salty hombres. However, Slade was also of the opinion that they would attend strictly to their own affairs so long as nobody interfered with them.

The bartender was not a Mexican. He was a

beady-eyed man with an oily smile and a fawning manner. The sort that evoluted from the snake rather than from the monkey.

A trio lounging against the bar to his left interested Slade. One was a hulking man with thick shoulders and abnormally long arms. He had a fleshy face and muddy little eyes set deep in rolls of fat. Beside him was a nondescript specimen, typical Border scum, lean and lanky. The third man was small and wiry. His eyes were black and bright and he looked intelligent, much more so than his two companions. Undoubtedly a ’breed, Indian blood predominating.

When Slade entered The Owl, the patrons had looked up, given him a swift, appraising glance and turned their attention elsewhere. Theirs was the expected reaction when a stranger entered such a place. But it seemed to Slade that the interest of the trio at the bar was different, more intense, although they appeared to be making an effort toward indifference.

There was a small cracked mirror behind the bar, and the three men were reflected in it. Slade, apparently absorbed in his drink, saw their lips move in an inaudible conversation. He was also sure that he saw them exchange significant glances with the unsavory bartender. Slade surveyed the room, but not for an instant did he let the three men out of his sight. A warning monitor in his brain was whispering that the trio spelled trouble and he had long ago learned not to ignore that subtle sixth sense which develops in men who ride alone with danger as a constant stirrup companion. Whatever move the trio might make, he was ready for it.

He was just a little surprised at the manner in which it was eventually made, something unusual for a Border country saloon on either side of the Line.

Slade had finished his second drink when the bartender shuffled forward with a bottle in his hand. "One on the house," he said unctuously. As he tipped the bottle the bulky man on Slade's left reached over and touched him on the shoulder.

As Slade half turned his head, the bartender began pouring the drink and at the same moment his left hand fleeted over the filling glass. The next instant he yelled in agony as slim fingers, like rods of steel, clamped his wrist. He yelled louder as the wrist was twisted sideways and up. From his paralyzed hand dropped a small vial that clattered on the bar spilling a few drops of a colorless liquid.

Simultaneously the three men on Slade's left went into action. Too simultaneously, in fact. They collided with one another as they rushed, hands pawing at their guns, and like the swoop of a giant hawk on a tangle of rabbits Slade was upon them. The smack of his fist against the small man's jaw resounded through the room.

The fellow went down as if he was shot and stayed where he fell, unconscious, blood pouring from his nose and mouth. The hulking man let out a roar that changed to a gurgling squawk as those terrible slim fingers closed on his throat. Right off his feet he was swung, his two hundred odd pounds handled as easily as if they had been so many ounces. Straight at the third man Slade hurled his ponderous bulk and the two hit the floor with a crash that shook the building. There they stayed, cowering, trying to flatten themselves into invisibility. And with good reason, for at them yawned a black gun muzzle, rock-steady, and the hammer of the gun was at full cock.

A second gun was in sight, too. It had materialized in Slade's left hand, apparently from nowhere. It twirled about his finger by the trigger guard, steadying momentarily with a snap and a jerk, its long barrel weaving from side to side and seeming to single out every man in the room for individual and particular attention. And the hammer of that gun was also at full cock!

The grandstand play was coldly calculated, and it got results, as Slade expected it would. The possibilities of that twirling Colt with the holder's forefinger rasping against the trigger at every turn were too much for the nerves of those in front of the black muzzle. They let out yells of expostulation, dodged behind tables or chairs or dived beneath them.

"Hold it, feller!" howled a fat man whose excess bulk protruded on either side of the thin post behind which he had sought safety. "Hold it! We ain't in on this. We—"

The twirling muzzle snapped rock-steady and gushed reddish flame. A blue trickle of smoke wisped up.

The fat man's howl ended in a strangled yelp that was echoed by a screech from the bartender as he reeled against the back-bar, blood spurting from his bullet-smashed hand, the gun he had snatched from beneath the bar clattering on the floor. He clutched wildly to save himself and snapped a shelf from its moorings. Down came a whole tier of bottles in a clang-jangling crash of smashing glass. The dizzying tang of spilled liquor blended with the raw, piercing smell of fresh blood and the fumes of burned powder.

Slade's voice blared through the uproar, "Anybody else interested in filling his hand? I aim to accommodate!"

Nobody appeared anxious to accept the invitation. The bartender sagged against the back bar, moaning and gagging amid a welter of blood, spilled alcohol and broken glass. The hulking man lay with his head resting in a spittoon and didn't move a finger, nor did his lanky companion. The small man lay unconscious.

Slade flicked a glance in their direction,

holstered his left gun and picked up the small vial from where it lay on the bar.

He sniffed it, his nostrils quivering a little. His eyes fixed on the cowering pair on the floor.

"Thought so," he remarked quietly, but in a voice that carried through the room. "Knockout drops, the kind that puts a man to sleep in a hurry, so that his friends can help him out and put him to bed—permanently." He flipped the tiny bottle into the air. Men jumped at the crash of a shot. There was a shower of bright fragments spinning and scintillating in the light, then a faint tinkle of bits of broken glass on the floor.

"Jumpin' sandtoads!" breathed a voice from somewhere. "That's shootin'!"

Slade's glance flickered over the room. Satisfied that his audience was impressed, he turned back to the three men on the floor.

"Get up," he gestured to the pair who retained their senses.

They scrambled erect, shrinking, fearful. Slade speculated them with his cold gaze. "Turn around," he ordered. They obeyed and he plucked their guns from the holsters and tossed them into a corner.

"Belly up to the bar," he told the big man.

The fellow did so, hesitant, wondering. Slade pointed to the brimming glass.

"Have one on the house," he said softly.

The man wet his dry lips with the tip of his

quivering tongue. His face was livid, his eyes dilated.

"I—I don't care special for tequila," he mumbled. "I'll—I'll have—have—"

"Tequila's a mighty good drink—for some folks," Slade said, his eyes pale flames in his bronzed face. "That's the kind of a drink that keeps some folks from catching lead poisoning—if they drink it quickly enough."

The other trembled still more at the deadly threat in Slade's soft voice. He stared at the black gun-muzzle, which had once more steadied in his direction. With a trembling hand he reached for the glass.

"Don't spill any of it," Slade cautioned.

The man raised the glass, his hand shaking as if with ague. He glanced desperately about the deathly silent room where men sat rigid, staring. His eyes came back to the gun and he saw that the trigger was pulled all the way back, with only Slade's thumb keeping the hammer from falling, and as he stared the thumb began to slide back on the milled surface toward the smooth tip. With a gagging moan he raised the glass and gulped its contents. Then he sagged against the bar, gripping the wood with both hands, his knuckles whitening with strain. Slowly the minutes passed.

Slade said nothing, but his eyes never left the drinker's face. The room was tense, without sound or motion, enthralled by the grisly drama.

A long sigh went up as the big man began to sway on his feet. His eyes were glazing, the lines of his face loosening; his breath whistled forth with a stertorous, rasping sound. One hand loosened its hold on the bar, pawed back frantically, the fingers coiling and writhing, fell away as if utterly weary. For a moment the other retained its grip, supporting the man's sagging weight, then it, too, slipped, fell limp. And just as limply the man sank in a huddled heap before the bar, breathing in choking gasps, his half-closed lids showing a glint of his glazed eyes.

TWELVE

SLADE TURNED TO THE SILENT WATCHERS. For a tense moment the only sound was the harsh breathing of the sleeper and the moaning sob of the wounded bartender.

"Anybody have any doubts as to what was in that little bottle?" Slade asked.

"Why, the mangy sons of hydrophobia skunks!" shouted a hard-eyed young cowboy who, with a company of his fellows, occupied a table by the dance floor.

Instantly, as if the shout had touched off hidden triggers of sound, the whole place was in an uproar, each man seemingly bent on voicing his disapproval more emphatically than his neighbor. The dealers at a couple of gambling tables wagged their heads and scowled impartially at the drugged sleeper and the moaning bartender to indicate that they had no part in the business.

Slade smiled thinly, but made no other comment. Abruptly he stooped and without effort picked up the limp body of the man who had received his crashing blow on the jaw and tucked him under his left arm. He still held the cocked gun in his right hand.

The bartender let out a louder moan. "Feller, can't I go?" he pleaded. "I need a doctor."

"You can go after I do, but not too soon after or you'll need more than a doctor," Slade answered grimly. He backed to the door as he spoke, paused to add significantly, "And I've a notion it would be a good idea for everybody to stay right where they are for a little while. I've got business to attend to and I don't hanker for company."

"That's right, feller," shouted the young cowhand. "Don't mess up the place. Take him outside and kill him."

Slade suppressed a chuckle as the doors swung shut after him. He felt pretty sure that his somewhat theatrical performance would have the desired effect and keep the crowd indoors for the few minutes he needed.

Nevertheless he wasted no time forking Shadow, swinging the unconscious form across the pommel and sending the big black racing along the dusty street.

"Thought so!" he muttered as a gun banged and a slug whistled past. "Some sidewinder's gotten up enough nerve to try a little fanging." He leaned low in the saddle as the gun cracked a second time, but now he was well past the outskirts of the town and didn't even hear the bullet.

"Sift sand, jughead," he told Shadow. "I don't think anybody will follow us, but we'll take no chances. Put space between us and that nest of snakes!"

The little breed was moaning and gurgling with returning consciousness. With his tie rope, Slade deftly bound his wrists behind him, and with the slack secured his ankles. He slapped him sharply on the back as he started to struggle.

"Quiet, or I'll put you to sleep again," he warned, repeating the injunction in Spanish. The fellow subsided with an incoherent mumble. Slade knew he couldn't be very comfortable in the position he was but figured he could stand it for a few more miles.

Not till he was beyond the desert country, with no signs of pursuit, and in a region where there were thickets and scattered groves did Slade slacken Shadow's pace. A little later he sighted a stand of trees and chaparral that would be suitable for what he had in mind. He veered Shadow into the grove, drawing rein beneath a large tree with thick growth on all sides. He dismounted and dumped his helpless prisoner on the ground.

There was plenty of dry wood ready to hand and Slade soon had a fire going. The flames shed plenty of light over the immediate surroundings, and flickered on the huge boughs of the tree. He got his sixty-foot manilla and tossed the noosed end over a convenient branch, letting the noose dangle within reach of his hand. Then he drew the prisoner into the circle of firelight and for a moment stood studying him.

"Okay, hombre," he said, "who put you up to

that little trick you tried on me in the *cantina*?"

The breed glowered sullenly and was silent.

"All right," Slade said. "If you won't talk you're no good to me."

He jerked the fellow to his feet and slipped the noose around his neck, drawing it tight. With a steady pull he hauled him into the air kicking and writhing, his mouth gasping, his eyes bulging. He held him there till his face began to purple. Then he eased off on the rope and let him fall heavily to the ground, where he lay groaning and gulping.

Slade gave him time to get his wind back, then addressed him again. "Ready to talk?" he asked.

"I talk," the breed gasped, cowering against the ground.

Slade switched to Spanish which he reasoned the man understood best. "Then who was responsible for what was tried tonight?" he asked.

"El Dorado," mumbled the breed.

"The golden man, eh? Why do you call him that?"

"His hair, it is gold."

"I see," Slade nodded. "And you were to deliver me to him?"

"*Si*."

"And where is he now?"

"To the north," the breed replied.

"And what does he buy there?"

"He buys the *escopeta*, the cartridge."

"Rifles and ammunition, eh? Which he plans to smuggle into Mexico?"

"*Si.*"

"And by what route does he plan to smuggle them?" The breed hesitated, his face working. Slade fingered the rope suggestively.

"If I tell and he knows, I die," the breed said.

"He'll not know unless you tell him," Slade replied. The breed studied him a moment. "I believe you," he said at length. "By way of Skeleton Canyon and San Luis Pass, El Dorado takes the arms."

Slade nodded, not particularly surprised. "When?" he asked.

"That I know not," the breed replied, and Slade believed him.

"And you know not just where he is now?"

"Perhaps Tombstone, perhaps Benson, perhaps Tucson. That, *Capitan*, is all I know."

Again Slade believed the fellow. He studied him for a moment, deciding that he didn't look particularly vicious and appeared more intelligent than average.

"*Muchacho*, why did you get mixed up with such a character as El Dorado?" he asked suddenly.

"He fights for the people," the breed replied simply.

"He does not," Slade instantly countered. "He is a murdering outlaw who thinks only of himself. Did he become the ruler of your land he would grind such as you as dirt beneath his feet. Your lot would be even worse than it is now, and I know that now it is not good."

The breed regarded him for a moment, his black eyes inscrutable. Then he said, "*Capitan*, when you speak, it is hard for one not to believe."

Slade reached down and flipped the noose from around the breed's neck. Another moment and he had freed wrists and ankles. The little man sat up, trying to rub some circulation back into his numbed members.

"You do not intend to kill me?" he asked wonderingly.

"Why should I?" Slade returned. "You have just been a fool in the hands of a smarter man. Nothing so terrible about that. He's fooled me a couple of times, too."

The breed grinned, and his dark face was almost attractive.

"Where are you from, *muchacho*?" Slade asked.

"From Sinaloa, far to the south."

"Go back there," Slade advised. "Till the soil or tend the *ganado*. Someday a man who is to be trusted will arise and really fight for the people and free them. When he does, follow him. I reckon now you can make your way back to Naco and get your horse without trouble. Then ride south. Here's your gun."

The breed took it, and again gazed wonderingly at Slade. "*Capitan*, you do not fear I will turn it on you?"

"No, I don't think you will," Slade smiled.

The little man thrust the big Colt into its sheath. He stood up, a bit shakily, rubbed his throat and his swollen jaw.

"*Capitan*," he said, "I will do as you say. And in days to come when I am tempted to do that which is wrong, I will think of you and forbear."

He turned and plunged into the growth. Slade listened until the sounds of his progress had dimmed in the distance. Then he turned to Shadow.

"Horse," he said, "I believe we did a pretty good night's work."

THIRTEEN

THE GROVE WAS AS GOOD A PLACE TO SLEEP as any, so Slade got the rig off Shadow and after smoking a cigarette spread his blanket beside the dying fire. He was awake at dawn and after a hearty breakfast cooked from the provisions he carried in his saddle pouches, he set out on his nearly seventy-mile ride to Skeleton Canyon.

While Walt Slade was having an interesting time along the Mexican Border, Wyatt Earp was embroiled in a misadventure so grotesquely embarrassing that ever afterward he would flush crimson with anger when he happened to recall it.

Because of the scarcity of water in the Tombstone section the stamp mills of the Tombstone Mining and Milling Company were located at Charleston on the west bank of the San Pedro River. Day and night the air of Charleston quivered to the pound and thunder of the great stamps doing their ceaseless dance. Upright rods of iron as large as a man's ankle, and heavily shod with a mass of steel and iron at their lower ends, were framed together like a gate, and these rose and fell, one after another, in an iron box called a battery. Each stamp weighed six-hundred pounds and more. The ore was shoveled into the battery and the steady dance of the stamps pulverized the rock to powder while a stream of water trickling into the battery turned this into a creamy paste. The minutest particles were driven through a fine wire screen that fitted close around the battery box. The particles were washed into great tubs, warmed by super-heated steam, called amalgamating pans. The mass of pulp in the pans was kept constantly stirred by mullers. A quantity of quicksilver was always kept in the battery, and this seized some of the liberated gold and silver particles and held onto them as did the quicksilver which was shaken into the pans, in a fine shower, about every half hour through a buckskin sack. Quantities of coarse salt and sulphate of copper were added from time to time to assist in the process of amalgamation by destroying the base metals which coated the gold and silver and prevented it from uniting with the quicksilver.

At the end of the week the machinery was stopped and the pulp was taken out of the pans and the batteries. The quicksilver with its imprisoned precious metal was molded into balls which were put into an iron retort that had a pipe leading from it to a container of water. A roasting heat was applied to the retort. The quicksilver turned to vapor, an oily black smoke that escaped through the pipe into the container where the water turned it into quicksilver again. From the retort was taken a lump of pure silver, white and frosty looking, with a gold content that did not show in the coloring. This was melted down and poured into a mold to produce a solid brick of silver weighing around two hundred and fifty pounds.

An intricate and tedious process, but the result was something to cause the mouths of road agents to water.

The bricks were shipped by wagon to Benson where they were loaded on the railroad. The Wells Fargo Express Company handled the shipments which in consequence came under Wyatt Earp's jurisdiction.

Somebody with brains and ingenuity evolved a scheme by which the wealth of silver might be transferred to the hands of gentlemen of easy morals who had an eye on it. The plan must have involved the services of some puddlers—men who cast the silver into bricks—who were not averse to making a crooked dollar.

A shipment of silver bricks left for Benson early the morning that Walt Slade left his camp in the grove and headed for Skeleton Canyon seventy miles distant. Beside the driver perched a shotgun guard, more for show than anything else, for what outlaw would be so foolish as to try to make off with the ponderous ingots each two hundred and fifty pounds. His horse would be bogged down in less than a mile and a hard-riding posse would overtake him with little difficulty.

So it was a highly astonished guard and driver when from the brush where the road forked rode four masked men with the familiar command, "Hands up!"

The guard instinctively started to raise his shotgun. A tall and broad-shouldered man in the forefront shot him. Strange to say, he did not kill him but only wounded him in the arm. The shotgun clattered to the roadway as the guard clutched at the injured member with a cry of pain. The more discreet driver was already "up," both hands reaching hard for the sky.

"Down off that and help unload," the tall masked man ordered.

The driver obeyed with alacrity. The groaning guard also clambered painfully from the seat. The tall leader of the robbers motioned him to one side. "You're good for nothing but to beller," he said. "Shut up! You're no more than scratched." He raised his voice in a shout, "Okay, Wes, bring it out!"

A light wagon drawn by two horses clattered from concealment. It was driven by a fifth masked man.

All except the watchful leader dismounted and went to work on the shipment. Grunting and swearing, they transferred the hefty and precious ingots to the wagon. Then with a cheerful goodbye to guard and driver, they headed the vehicle down the fork of the trail that trended due south to the Mexican Border. Where the trail curved through tall brush, one of the outlaws turned off a moment, to reappear leading a fifth horse, saddled and bridled.

The wounded guard was still cursing and groaning, but the driver was all excitement. "Tom!" he exclaimed, "the devils forgot to shoot the horses! Wait, I'll tie a rag round that arm—it's just a meat wound—and then I'm heading to town. I'll get Wyatt Earp and a bunch and they'll run the hellions down before they get across the Line."

Suiting the action to the word, he cut loose one of the stage horses, mounted it bareback and sent it speeding for Tombstone. Ten minutes after the driver rode his lathered mount into the silver city Wyatt Earp and his posse were on the trail.

In addition to the three Earps, Wyatt, Morgan and Virgil, the posse included Doc Holliday and Buckskin Frank Leslie, both staunch Earp men. In the light of what followed, Wyatt could not have made a more unfortunate selection.

The posse sighted the light wagon from the crest of a rise no great distance from the scene of the holdup. It was standing at the bottom of the long slope and nearly two miles away. The eagle-eyed Wyatt counted five men grouped around it. Over to one side stood a clump of saddled and bridled horses.

"Looks like the blasted wind spiders are having trouble of some sort," Wyatt exclaimed exultantly. "Let's go!"

At top speed they thundered down the slope. Soon it became apparent that their approach was noted by the outlaws. The white blobs of faces turned in their direction. There was a drawing together of heads, then a concerted rush for the horses. A moment later and the last owlhoot had vanished into the brush. The wagon heaped with the metal ingots still stood motionless, looking very small and lonely in the vast desolation.

Minutes later the posse pulled their blowing horses to a halt beside the wagon.

"A wheel came off," Wyatt exclaimed. "Reckon they had to hunt for the hub cap—there it is lying in the road where they dropped it."

"We riding after the horned toads?" Morgan asked excitedly. Wyatt shook his head.

"Guess not," he decided. "They've got a head-start and the chances are they know the lay of the land, which we don't. Mighty little chance of catching them up, and they might manage to lose us in that badland over there, circle back and grab off the wagon. No, we'll take the stuff back to Charleston. Now I wonder what loco hellions tried this fool trick, anyhow?"

"Who else but the Brocius bunch?" said Holliday.

"Don't you believe it," Wyatt answered. "Trust John Ringo and Curly Bill not to make such a fool try. It was some brush poppin' outfit with mighty little savvy. Even if their wagon hadn't busted up we'd have caught them before they made the Line. If it had been the Brocius bunch there wouldn't have been any horses left alive for the driver to ride to town. Mighty good chance neither the driver nor the guard would have been left alive, for that matter. Brocius and Ringo don't fool when they're on a job. But even if the driver hadn't gotten to town, Benson would have been getting suspicious when the stage didn't show up on time and we would still have had time to overtake that wagon before it got across the Border and in the clear down there. No, Brocius would never have mixed up in such a loco scheme."

"The driver swore he recognized Curly Bill's voice," insisted the argumentative Holliday.

"He thought he recognized it," corrected Wyatt. "It's got so that whenever something is pulled in this section everybody recognizes Curly Bill in one way or another, even if Bill is fifty miles away sitting in the middle of town with folks all around him. It's got to be a habit with guards and drivers. Screw that hub cap in place, Morg, and be sure the nut under it is tight, and we'll head back to town. We did a good chore. The mill manager will get a surprise."

The mill manager did, but not exactly as Wyatt figured.

With Morgan driving the wagon the posse made a triumphant entry into Charleston. The mill manager bustled out to greet them, smiling and rubbing his hands together. He shook hands with Wyatt, congratulated him on his exploit. Then he turned to the wagon to check the tally of the recovered bricks.

Suddenly he halted, staring. His face turned purple, he seemed to breathe with difficulty. His eyes glared and watered as he turned to the puzzled posse members, who were noting these alarming symptoms with considerable concern. But he did not address them directly at the moment. He beckoned a group of laborers busy nearby.

"Unload that stuff, carry it into my office and stack it," he ordered in a choked voice.

The laborers obeyed, struggling with the unwieldy ingots that seemed to be uncommonly heavy. When the last brick was deposited, the manager motioned the posse into his office. He closed and locked the door, then he exploded.

"Lead!" he roared. "What's the idea, anyhow? Lead!"

The posse stared in bewilderment. "Lead?" Wyatt Earp repeated. "What the devil you talking about, Austin?"

"Lead!" stormed the manager. "Bars of lead frosted with a little white paint to make it look like silver. Any fool with one eye could see that! That is," he added with meaning, "if he was honest."

For once Wyatt Earp was taken aback. His jaw dropped. He blinked at the wrathful manager. The other's implication struck home and he flushed angrily.

"Austin, are you trying to say that ain't silver?"

"Yes, I'm trying to say that ain't silver!" the manager mimicked with vicious sarcasm.

Wyatt Earp's face darkened even more. "And you're intimating that—" he began.

"I'm intimating nothing," the manager interrupted. "I'm telling you that thousands of dollars worth of silver is missing and in place of it you bring me a wagonload of rubbish worth a few cents a pound. How in the devil do you think we are going to explain this to Wells Fargo and collect our insurance? They'll fight us through every court in the land and beat us."

Wyatt was speechless. He examined the bricks closely, cut into one with his knife. There was no gainsaying the manager; it was a patent fact, the bars were lead.

"Looks like it was the Brocius bunch, after all," Doc Holliday observed.

Wyatt turned on him with an oath. "Brocius bunch, blazes!" he exploded. "Neither Curly Bill nor any of his gang has the brains to figure out a scheme like this. It was planned and executed by a man smarter than all the Brocius bunch put together. Let's get out of here!"

The crestfallen posse filed out, followed by the black looks of the plainly suspicious manager.

Outside, Wyatt Earp paused, glaring at the empty wagon. "Yes, a hellion with brains," he said. "And there's only one man I've talked with lately that I figure has the brains to engineer such a deal."

"That El Halcon feller is considerable of a jigger," Doc Holliday commented cheerfully.

"I didn't mention El Halcon," Wyatt growled.

"Nope," agreed Holliday, "but I still think he's considerable of a jigger. Incidentally, he rode out of town a couple of days back and ain't been seen since. Wonder where he rode to?"

"To the devil I hope!" snorted Wyatt. "Yes, he's smart, but I'll drop a loop on him yet, see if I don't."

"Better tie hard and fast when you do," advised Holliday. "Don't take a chance on a dally. When a dally slips off the horn, sometimes the feller holding the end of the rope gets stood on his ear."

Wyatt set his jaw grimly and did not reply to Holliday's malicious needling. Without a word he turned his horse toward Tombstone.

The story got around—the mine manager saw to that—and Tombstone roared. Even those friendly to Wyatt Earp had to chuckle over the ludicrous affair. And those who were not friendly were, like the mine manager, suspicious. Doc Holliday and Frank Leslie were members of the posse, were they not? Just the Earps, and Doc Holliday and Buckskin Frank Leslie.

All in all, the debacle on the Benson Road didn't do the Earp faction a bit of good.

FOURTEEN

IT WAS LATE AFTERNOON of his second day of riding when Walt Slade drew near the west mouth of Skeleton Canyon. Above him towered high hills of red rock with only a few miles farther on the main range of the Peloncillos. Across the valley to the west gloomed the Chiricahuas and he could see the far-off shadowy mouth of Silver Creek Canyon that led to Paradise and Curly Bill Brocius' headquarters at Galeyville. Skeleton Creek flashed and dimpled in the sunlight. Nearby was a spring hidden in the cliffs where in summers of drought when all the streams were dry the Indians always found plenty of clear, cold water.

Slade knew that for a long time smuggler trains, coming up from Mexico by way of San Luis Pass through the Animas range and across the Animas Valley in New Mexico, had threaded the gorges of Skeleton on their way to the San Simon Valley. Usually they would turn north through the San Simon, round the northern end of the Chiricahuas, and passing through Dragoon Gap and across the San Pedro arrive in Santa Cruz Valley, where they would pitch camp among the cholla thickets in the environs of Tucson. There they would wait until merchants who dealt in contraband came out to barter.

Going north the pack saddles borne by mules mostly carried Mexican silver dobe dollars. On the southward trip they would bulge with goods and commodities of many kinds. In Murray De Spain's case the *aparejos* could be expected to contain rifles and cartridges. Or at least so Slade figured. How he was to drop a loop on the elusive De Spain, Slade had not the least notion at the moment, but he had decided it would be well to give the route so often followed by the smuggler trains a careful once-over. Perhaps in sinister Skeleton Canyon he would be able to discover something that might tend to simplify the task.

Before he had penetrated far into the desolate gorge, Slade was ready to concede that Skeleton Canyon was rightly named. Everywhere there were bones, among the flowers that enameled the banks of the stream with vivid hues, scattered through the grass in dismal abundance, protruding from the soil, lying in the shadow of boulders. Fragments and shards, and here and there almost whole skeletons, some of them unpleasantly recent. The men killed in Skeleton Canyon were left unburied to fill the bellies of coyote and buzzard, with the busy ants to polish clean what tooth and beak could not pulverize. Grisly relics of battle, massacre and murder, they gleamed white under the noonday sun or glowed with the ghostly light of phosphorescence when the stars peered into the dark depths between the towering walls of stone. Here for years without number men had fought and died, leaving behind these sad mementos to the frailty of human life.

He had ridden but a short distance into the canyon when Shadow's front foot struck something that bounded across the trail and came to rest against a stone, grinning toothily. It was a human skull. Nearby gleamed the broken arch of a rib. The infernal place was sown with bones!

It was almost full dark when he passed the tall cathedral spires, a grouping of chimney rocks that formed what was known as the Devil's Kitchen. Slade chuckled as he recalled the story of two terrified cowboys who vowed they had seen a ring of skeletons dancing in the Devil's Kitchen, the moonlight shining through their ribs. Slade was of the opinion that these terpsichorean skeletons had materialized from a bottle, but amid such grisly surroundings, anything seemed possible.

Somewhere in the deepening gloom a shriek sounded, a shrill, shivery crescendo that sobbed and pulsed and died in an eerie wail. Just the hunting call of a prowling cougar.

Another cry sounded, higher-pitched than the first, tremulous, lonely. A catamount gliding among the rocks, but the varmint sounded different from the ordinary garden variety of the pests. Bats flitted to and fro across the trail, emitting their sharp needle-like note. A night hawk almost brushed his face with its wings and uttered an unearthly scream. An owl swooped past on silent pinons, spirit-like in the gloom. Soon Slade reached a spot where the creek widened to form a stretch of marsh, and over the dark bog a pale light glowed and flickered, wandering here and there, restless, tossing. A will-o'-the-wisp, of course. A little wind in the upper branches of the trees was like voices babbling, and the creek, murmuring along, seemed to be trying to tell him something in some strange language he couldn't understand.

Slade was beginning to understand why it was said you couldn't find a Mexican in the country with nerve enough to ride through Skeleton Canyon after dark. Ghosts! Of course there was no such thing. Arrant nonsense, the vagaries conjured up by superstitious minds. Ghosts! Bosh!

The cougar wailed again. An owl on some blasted pine answered with a note like to a human whimper of agony. Another marsh light tossed and flickered over the bog he had just passed. Above, something huge and dark blotted out the stars for an instant and was gone. No doubt a belated condor-vulture braving the night. But why did it leave that faint sighing in its wake? Just the air displaced by giant pinons? Ghosts!

What man, endowed with a reasoning mind, could allow himself to think, let alone believe in such folly? Yet all at once, like an enemy from the dark, old stories leaped at him. Old tales of spectres grim and bloody, of goblins, and haunted houses from whose dim desolation strange sounds would come; tales long since heard, and forgot—till now.

Ghosts! Why, the trail was full of them. They crowded upon his heels, they peered over his shoulders; he felt them brush his elbows, and heard them gibbering at him from the shadows! He laughed aloud at his own conceit, and the laugh flung back from the cliffs in a ghoulish cachinnation.

And then abruptly he heard something that turned amusement into concern, a sound never made by a disembodied spectre conjured up by an over-active imagination, a faint clicking somewhere ahead, a mere staccato whispering, distant, but loudening. He pulled Shadow to a halt to listen better. And as he did so, he heard a similar sound far to the rear.

"Horse," he muttered, "we're smack in between two bunches riding toward us from different directions. Chances are they're only some cowpokes cutting across from one valley to the other, but funny things have happened in this infernal hole. Guess we'd better play it safe."

He glanced about. Dimly seen in the starlight

was a tall and broad butte that flanked the trail less than a dozen yards distant. Its base was shrouded in thick gloom. He twitched the bridle and sent Shadow pacing toward this dubious sanctuary. He was pretty sure that nobody passing along on the trail could see him and he counted on Shadow, usually a very silent horse, not to make a noise that would betray his presence.

The sensible thing to do, he had to admit, was ride on across the gorge and put some distance between himself and the trail, but he was intensely curious as to who those night riders might be and what their business in the unsavory canyon was. Pulling Shadow to a halt he sat motionless, peering and listening.

The beat of hoofs steadily loudened. From the west it was a sprightly rattle, from the east, much closer, a slower, more monotonous plodding. Apparently neither troop could hear the approach of the other above the racket made by their own mounts.

Abruptly Slade saw, to the east, dimly outlined by the starshine reflecting from the cliffs, a long string of grotesque shapes with monstrously bulging sides. He quickly identified them as mules bearing well plumped-out *aparejos* or pack sacks. Riding by the side of the train were horsemen. Like distorted spectres they drifted past his hiding place, hoofs thudding, bridle irons jingling. The last horseman riding behind the train had passed the butte when all fire broke loose. There was a shout of alarm followed by the crack of a shot, then a regular drum roll of gunfire.

Yells, curses, howls of pain, the snorting and screaming of frightened horses, the clashing of hoofs and the braying of mules all rose in a hideous pandemonium. Back and forth spurted red flashes, cleaving the dark, luridly lighting the scene for split seconds, revealing a mad welter of mules and horsemen struggling, shifting, swirling about.

For perhaps a third of a minute the uproar continued. Then Slade dimly saw a group of horsemen wheel their mounts and go streaking back the way they had come, followed by vengeful bullets.

It had been a lively shindig while it lasted and the explanation was obvious. A band of horsemen riding east from the San Simon Valley had rammed into a smuggling train coming up from the south. Evidently they had gotten the worst of the encounter and were sifting sand for safety.

With the smuggling train all was still confusion. Men were swearing exasperated oaths in English and Spanish as they tried to straighten out the tangle. Some of the mules had bolted sideways from the trail. Others had shifted their loads which hung crazily against their bellies. Curses loud and deep arose, mingled with the groans of wounded men. A torch flared, and another. Slade could see men on foot moving about, apparently trying to ascertain the extent of the damage. Others were straightening the tilted pack sacks and quieting the nervous mules. One or two were peering at motionless shapes on the ground.

Slade sat tense and silent, leaning forward and ready to grip Shadow's nose should the big black take a notion to neigh. He knew he was in deadly danger. Should the smugglers spot him they would very likely open fire at once. He swiftly calculated his chances were he forced to make a break for it and evolved a plan of action.

To the west the trail was hopelessly blocked by the horses and mules. To the east the way was open, with a bulge of chimney rock less than fifty yards distant. His only hope would be to make for that and whisk around the bulge. With that much start there would be scant chance, barring accidents, of anybody overtaking Shadow. His nerves strained taut as piano wire, he waited, hoping that he might escape discovery.

That hope, however, was not to be realized. A man bearing a torch had come down the trail a little ways, peering about. He raised the torch on high. It blazed up brightly and as the man turned his head he saw Slade outlined in the glare. His startled shout shot the Ranger into action.

"Trail, Shadow, trail!" he roared.

The great black bounded forward. Straight at

the man with the torch Slade sent him. He tried to duck the avalanche of flesh and bone hurtling toward him but Shadow struck him with his shoulder and swept him aside. The torch flew from his hand as he hit the ground and sputtered out. A storm of shouts and questions arose, then a crackling of guns. Bullets whizzed past Slade. One ripped his sleeve. A second flicked a patch of leather from his left boot and almost paralyzed his leg with the force of the blow. Bending low in the saddle he urged Shadow to greater speed. Slade heard a clatter of hoofs in pursuit, but in another instant he had whipped around the bulge and the hullabaloo behind swiftly died to a drone in the distance. Settling himself in the hull, he leaned over and tried to massage some feeling back into his leg. Satisfied that no particular damage had been done, he straightened up and gave his attention to riding.

"Well, Shadow, it's open to debate as to whether there are ghosts in Skeleton Canyon," he observed, "but it's sure for certain that things as bad or even worse do maverick around in this blasted crack. In fact, a nice sociable ghost or two right now would be a welcome relief. June along, horse, we've got to do some travelling before we hole up for the night."

FIFTEEN

THEY DID DO SOME TRAVELLING, almost to the east mouth of the canyon, before Slade decided he could risk calling a halt. He made a fireless camp under the overhang of a cliff and, in defiance of the ghosts, slept soundly. At daybreak he cooked a rather scanty meal from what remained of his provisions and over his after-breakfast cigarette reviewed the night's happenings and debated what effect they might have on his future movements.

The smuggler train was a big one and very likely the *aparejos* were crammed with Mexican silver. Was it intended to pay for the arms the breed from Sinaloa said Murray De Spain was collecting for shipment to Mexico? Slade thought the assumption not beyond the realm of probability.

Carrying the argument a bit further, was it not logical to assume that De Spain would be somewhere around Tucson to superintend the loading of the arms, and possibly would accompany the train on its return trip to Mexico? Slade thought that also quite possible.

All guesswork, of course, but the first thing resembling a lead to the elusive outlaw's whereabouts he had been able to unearth.

If his deductions were correct, the train had a long trip ahead of it, and it would not be able to make any great speed. That should give him plenty of time to try and evolve a plan by which he might put to use what he had learned. Just how, he as yet had not the slightest notion. Pinching out his cigarette he saddled up and rode east until he reached the point where the canyon emptied into the Animas Valley. He pulled up and studied the terrain ahead.

From where he sat his horse he could see, far to the southeast across the valley, the mouth of San Luis Pass, the wide low gap through the Animas range between the Playas and Animas valleys. After a prolonged inspection, Slade decided that if he were to make a play for De Spain in this section, Skeleton Canyon would be his best bet. Neither the valley nor the pass appeared favorable. He turned Shadow and started on his long ride back to Tombstone from which there was an easy route to Tucson some fifty miles to the northwest of the silver city.

Slade found no fresh bones in Skeleton Canyon. If anybody had been killed during the wild foray of the night before, the smugglers had disposed of the bodies.

Darkness had fallen when Slade reached Tombstone the following day. After caring for his horse, his first thought was something to eat. He decided the Crystal Palace, noted for good food, would do as well as any. When he entered the saloon he saw John Ringo standing at the bar. The outlaw waved a greeting and a little later strolled over to the table where Slade was eating.

"Mind if I sit down?" he asked courteously.

Slade waved him to a chair and Ringo dropped into it and began rolling a cigarette.

"Suppose you heard about what happened to Wyatt Earp?" he asked.

Slade hadn't and Ringo proceeded to regale him with an account of the fiasco on the Benson road. He apparently took a huge delight in Wyatt Earp's discomfiture and his somber face grew animated as he talked.

"There are folks who figure Curly Bill had something to do with it," he observed. "But I happen to know he didn't. When he heard about it he spent most of the day cussin' because he didn't think of that little trick. I guess Wyatt is fit to be hogtied and I don't wonder. I hate his guts but I admire his ability. It isn't often somebody puts something over on Wyatt. I've a notion if he ever gets his hand on the jigger who did it he'll eat him raw without salt. Well, be seeing you. I haven't had a drink for ten minutes and I'm getting thirsty." With a nod he rose and sauntered back to the bar.

Slade thought about what he had learned. His prophecy that the peace officers of Cochise County were in for stirring times had been no idle prediction; Murray De Spain was setting up in business.

There was no doubt in Slade's mind as to who had planned and executed the fantastic scheme. It had all the earmarks of a De Spain coup. Although his sympathies were with Wyatt Earp, he had to chuckle as he thought of the cold rage which must be afflicting the famous frontier marshal. Yes, Wyatt was fit to be hogtied, all right.

However, when he visited the Oriental Bar a little later, Wyatt showed no signs of perturbation. He was standing at the far end of the bar, as usual, accompanied by his brothers Virgil and Morgan and Doc Holliday. He caught Slade's eye and composedly nodded a greeting.

The bar was crowded and Slade found an empty table and ordered a drink, his glance roving over the big room and for the moment discovering nothing of outstanding interest. He was not particularly surprised when Wyatt Earp approached and occupied a vacant chair on the opposite side of the table.

"Been out of town a few days, haven't you?" Wyatt asked.

"That's right," Slade admitted. "Took a little ride down to the south."

Wyatt Earp nodded. Abruptly he shot out a question, "Know anything about silver, Slade?"

"Enough to tell it from lead," Slade smiled in reply.

Wyatt Earp flushed slightly and Slade saw his right hand ball into a fist. But when he spoke his voice was casually quiet. “Didn’t happen to cut around north by way of the Benson road when you rode back, did you?”

Slade’s eyes danced with laughter. “Earp,” he said, “I’ve always heard you were an outstanding peace officer, and I believe you are, but as a detective you are a dismal failure. Your approach lacks subtlety. And never ask a direct question, except as a tactical surprise.”

Wyatt Earp’s jaw dropped slightly. He stared at Slade, shook his head. “A feller needs a dictionary to keep up with you,” he declared. “You ought to meet up with that feller who told us you were headed this way. He slings the same sort of palaver you do.”

“What fellow is that?” Slade asked.

“A feller who stopped off here on his way to the San Pedro Valley,” Wyatt replied. “Said his name was De Spain, I believe.”

Slade leaned forward, and even the intrepid marshal drew back a little before the sudden cold glitter of his eyes.

“How was that again?” Slade said softly. “Did you say his name was De Spain? Murray De Spain?”

“Yes, I believe that was it, Murray De Spain,” Wyatt answered, and abruptly he understood.

“So that’s the feller you’re after?” he said.

"Yes, that's the man I'm after," Slade replied, adding as he stood up, "And the man who made a fool of you on the Benson road. Good night!"

For some moments after Slade had taken his departure, Wyatt Earp sat gazing at the swinging doors. He got slowly to his feet and walked back to where Doc Holliday and the others were awaiting him in expectant silence. Wyatt ordered a drink and downed it at a gulp. He wiped his drooping mustache and shook his head.

"I don't know what to make of that feller!" he declared, voicing a complaint made by more than one Texas peace officer. "No, I don't know what to make of him, but I do know one thing. Gentlemen, I don't believe I'm exactly a coward, and I never was much on running, but if I was in that De Spain hellion's boots, I'd sprout wings and fly fast and far!"

Outside the Oriental, Slade paused uncertainly. He had left Wyatt Earp so abruptly in order to get control of his own boiling anger before conversing further with the marshal. Murray De Spain had scored again!

"Seems whenever I think I'm on that hellion's trail I find that instead he's in behind, stalking me," he growled morosely to an unresponsive street lamp.

Slade did not think that De Spain had accomplished much by notifying Wyatt Earp that El Halcon was on his way to Tombstone, but the shrewd devil's uncanny ability to unerringly deduce what he had in mind was enough to aggravate a saint. His anger blazed up again at thought of it. Then abruptly he realized the humor of the situation and he chuckled even as he had chuckled at the thought of Wyatt Earp's fury over what happened to him on the Benson road. It appeared, he reflected ruefully, that he and Wyatt were in precisely the same corral, with Murray De Spain twirling the loop.

He began to wonder about John Ringo's frustrated attempt to pick a row with him in the Crystal Palace. Had De Spain taken Bill Brocius and his bunch into camp and handed them the chore of eliminating him? After more sober reflection, he was inclined to doubt the correctness of the supposition. Ringo was an intelligent man, and an intelligent man would hardly have employed so crude and clumsy an approach.

But one thing was incontrovertible: Wyatt Earp was now definitely suspicious of him, and whether that would work to his advantage was problematical. The grim marshal was a bad man to have aligned against one, and a mistaken expert can sometimes do irreparable damage.

Deciding he had had enough for one day, he went to bed.

Slade spent the following day in Tombstone, desiring to give Shadow a good rest. That night he strolled about the town, visiting various places but learning nothing of value. On the morning of the second day he rode north by west on the Benson road, his destination Tucson and its environs. And Wyatt Earp watched him go.

Wyatt Earp had little doubt but that Slade really was on the trail of the man who called himself Murray De Spain, but he was far from convinced that the mysterious wanderer called El Halcon was not the tall masked outlaw who had directed operations when the silver robbery was pulled on the Benson road. He again questioned the driver and guard, endeavoring to glean a more detailed description of the outlaw leader.

"He was tall, all right, and big," said the driver. "I don't know what color his hair was, it may have been black or maybe he had it covered with that black cloth he wore over his face. I was sort of excited and didn't notice such things particular. But he was riding a bay horse, a dam good-looking critter, not a black."

"He wouldn't be riding a black," Wyatt grunted. "That black horse El Halcon forks stands out like a cowhand in church. Just about the finest animal I ever laid eyes on. Nobody with half a brain would ride such a cayuse when pulling a robbery. Chances are he had the black in reserve in case he had to really make a run for it."

"Could be," admitted the driver, "but I've a notion that bay would show heels to most anything in horse flesh that comes along."

SIXTEEN

SLADE RODE SLOWLY, for he wanted to study the country. He passed St. David, settled by Mormons a few years before, and forded the San Pedro River about ten miles farther on. Here in the San Pedro Valley, he knew, one of the strangest battles of the Southwest had occurred. Colonel Cooke and his Mormon Battalion were attacked by wild bulls. The fight started early in the morning and continued until noon when the attackers retreated after suffering some sixty of their number killed. A dozen or more men were wounded, some seriously, and the belligerent bulls managed to slay several mules. That had happened nearly forty years before, however, and he saw no descendants of the four-footed warriors.

The day was drawing to a close when he reached Benson on the bank of the San Pedro and close to mountains. In all directions were rolling lomas, mesas and escarpments cut and broken by erosion, the terrain being fully as rugged as that between St. David and the river crossing.

Benson had been founded not long before as the railroad town for Tombstone, but the area around the town had been inhabited for centuries. As early as 1697 the fertility and prosperity of the ranches along the San Pedro were mentioned by travellers.

The town, built along the trail, consisted mostly of arched and flat-topped adobes and frame false-fronted structures. These were filled with saloons, tinhorns, rustlers, hustlers, cribs and gambling dens. Cowboys, miners and Mexicans frequented the town and kept it lively.

Slade decided to spend the night in Benson, hoping to pick up some scraps of information. In a saloon he struck up an acquaintance with a young cowman who owned a ranch about midway between Benson and Tucson.

"I expect to be in Tucson myself in a couple of days," the rancher remarked after Slade had mentioned the Old Pueblo, Tucson's informal name, as his destination. "Maybe I'll run into you there if you're still sticking around. I usually hang out in the Ochoa saloon on Meyer Street. Keep an eye open for me." Slade promised to do so.

Slade left Benson early the following morning. Riding steadily, he covered the more than forty-five miles to the Old Pueblo by nightfall.

Tucson was a good deal of a town. Founded in 1700 by Padre Eusebio Kino, a Jesuit missionary, who built the mission of San Xavier del Bac on the site, it had long since outgrown its ancient adobe walls and was spreading out over the broad desert valley. Business had gained impetus with the discovery of silver and copper at Tombstone and Bisbee and the coming of the Southern Pacific Railroad. Its merchants grew rich in the smuggler trade and gentlemen of blunted conscience who had been forced to leave California and other sections found the climate salubrious.

Slade had no difficulty in locating the Ochoa saloon which his rancher friend in Benson mentioned, and found the drinks up to the average and the food excellent.

For three days he rode the surrounding country or strolled about the town, and learned nothing. Smuggler trains were conspicuous by their absence and he was unable to glean any information relative to the arrival or departure of one. Began to look like the one he met in Skeleton Canyon had been delayed.

The evening of the third day he encountered the young rancher in the Ochoa and they had dinner together.

"Funny thing happened when I left Benson," the rancher remarked in the course of the conversation. "Just outside of town I passed a whoppin' big smuggler train. They were loading the mules, and getting ready to pull out, I reckon. Sure were hard looking hombres, some white and some Mexican 'breeds. A lot of 'em; must have been twenty or twenty-five, more than needed to handle a train that size. Guess they were packing something mighty valuable and weren't taking any chances. A big tall jigger with yellow hair was superintending things and he sure gave me a close once-over as I rode past. Bad-looking eyes. Made me feel sort of funny between the shoulder blades till I got over the next rise. Sort of out of the ordinary to run into a train down there; they most always head for Tucson."

Slade drew a weary breath. De Spain had put it over again. Breaking precedent, he had arranged for his shipment to be delivered at Benson, for reasons best known to himself. While he, Slade, had been chasing his tail around Tucson, the train was rolling south. He wondered if he could catch up with the devils before they made it through Skeleton Canyon and the San Luis Pass to Mexico. Well, it would be worth trying; couldn't do any worse than he had been doing of late.

An hour before dawn found Slade in the saddle. It was seventy miles to Tombstone but Shadow, given an hour's rest now and then, could make the trip without laying over.

Slade rode at an easy pace that nevertheless ate up the miles. The Santa Catalinas flared scarlet and gold in the sunrise. The level rays flashed and glittered on the rugged Coronados and were slanted when he passed the Tanque Verdes on the east, with the Tucson mountains fading to purple shadows behind and to the west. He paused at Pantano for something to eat and to allow Shadow to feed and rest, then rode steadily until he reached Benson. Again he stopped for an hour, having covered nearly fifty miles. The sun was well down the western sky when he forded the San Pedro and rode on with Tombstone about sixteen miles distant; it would be dark when he reached the silver city. With still some ten or eleven miles to go he let the horse amble up a long rise, keeping him in the cooler shadow at the side of the trail. He reached the crest, glanced down the opposite sag and abruptly pulled Shadow to a halt.

Something was going on in the deep hollow below. At the bottom of the sag was a wide jumble of rocks and boulders. To the left a long slope flung upward to a wooded skyline. To the right was broken country studded with rocks, groves and bristles of thicket. And beyond the rocks the trail levelled off after topping a low rise to the south, the crest of which was only about thirty or forty yards from the lower level. Over to one side, concealed from the south by a thicket, Slade saw a clump of horses.

Behind the rocks, where the trail from the north levelled off nearly a dozen men were crouched, all facing south.

As if drawn up by invisible wires, five horsemen appeared on the crest of the low rise and rode down toward the crouching drygulchers.

In the foremost rider, tall, stalwart, the rays of the low lying sun glinting on his pale hair and mustache, Slade recognized, even at that distance—more than six hundred yards—no other than Wyatt Earp.

Evidently the marshal and his posse were riding after someone, and they were riding fast. Even as Slade instinctively tightened his grip on the reins, they reached the bottom of the sag.

From behind the rocks clouds of smoke mushroomed upwards. Slade saw two of the approaching horsemen topple to the ground. The three remaining, one of whom was Wyatt Earp, instantly flung themselves from their saddles and dived for shelter back of boulders flanking the trail. Smoke continued to fog up and Slade could hear the constant crackle of the guns.

Under the smoke cloud he sensed movement, the drygulched were fanning out on either side, undoubtedly with a view to out-flank the besieged posse.

Slade's hand dropped to the butt of the Winchester snugged in the saddle boot beneath his left thigh. No! That wouldn't do. The distance was too great. He might startle the drygulchers, possibly wing one, but a couple of riflemen would take care of him. To ride down the trail was just a convenient way to commit suicide. But something had to be done in a hurry if the beleaguered posse was to be saved from certain death.

He glanced to the left, surveying the upward flinging slope with all-seeing eyes. The growth was tall and thick; a horse and rider would be hidden, but some two hundred yards above where the drygulchers crouched, it thinned to scattered bushes interspersed by boulders and fangs of rock. Two hundred yards with practically no cover. However, Slade didn't hesitate. He sent Shadow into the growth, urging him forward through the bristling tangle.

But the going was bad and even the powerful black made slow progress. In the hollow below, the guns continued to crack as outlaws and lawmen exchanged shots. Slade tensed in dread anticipation of an abrupt ceasing of the fire, which would signify all was over.

After what seemed an eternity of nerve-tearing suspense, he reached the spot where the growth thinned. Pushing forward cautiously he gazed through a final straggle.

From where he sat his horse he had a clear view of everything going on in the hollow below. He could see Wyatt Earp and his companions crouching low, their glances shooting to right and left, their guns ready. And he could see that the drygulchers had almost completed their flanking movement. In another minute or two they would have the doomed trio at their mercy. Again Slade's hand dropped to his Winchester, but again he withdrew it. He might kill one or two, but those experienced outlaws would quickly realize that they had but one man to deal with and would blow him out of the hull.

But he must act quickly if the three men fighting a brave but losing battle were to be saved. There was but one thing to do, a wild gamble with death with all the odds against him. Again he did not hesitate. Dropping the reins on Shadow's neck he drew both guns and clamped his knees against the black's sides in a signal the big horse knew well.

SEVENTEEN

AS HE WATCHED EL HALCON ride out of Tombstone on the Benson road, Wyatt Earp was pretty well convinced that it was only a matter of time till some fresh atrocity would be reported. Nor did he have long to wait. Only five days, in fact. And again it happened on the Benson road. When the stage from Benson was almost in sight of Tombstone, three masked men stepped out of the mesquite. They shot and wounded the guard and a passenger and took the Wells-Fargo box containing the Sulphuret payroll money, nearly forty thousand dollars in gold and silver. Ordering the driver to continue on to Tombstone, they rode toward Benson.

The driver obeyed orders and got to Tombstone as quickly as he could, and reported the outrage.

Without an instant's delay, Wyatt Earp assembled a posse consisting of his brother Morgan, Doc Holliday, and two young cowboys, Bill Dunlap and Tom Brady.

"I've a notion I can outfox those devils," he told the others as they rode out of Tombstone at top speed. "They'll head for Tucson, sure as shooting. Once they get there they'll mix with the crowd in some saloon and there'll be a dozen to swear they'd been there for a week. But I know a shortcut the other side of the San Pedro crossing that should bring us to the trail ahead of them. If we get there first, and I figure we will, we'll bag the lot of them and recover the money, too."

The others were of the opinion that Wyatt had the right idea and pushed their horses for all they could give. About ten miles northwest of Tombstone they topped a rise and charged down the opposite sag toward a level stretch studded with huge boulders. As they reached the bottom of the slope they were met by a blaze of gunfire from men holed up behind the rocks.

Dunlap and Brady were instantly killed. Wyatt, Morgan and Holliday flung themselves to the ground and sought shelter. Both Morgan and Holliday were slightly wounded. Wyatt, as usual, was untouched.

But the grim marshal knew that the reprieve was brief. He could tell from the sound of the guns that they were greatly outnumbered. There was no place to run. Did they leave the little clump of sheltering rocks they would be instantly shot down. Looked like there was nothing to do but make as good an end as possible. Bullets were spatting against the boulders and Wyatt saw that the angle from which the shots were coming was slowly but steadily widening. He knew very well what that meant.

"Looks like this is it, boys," he calmly

observed. "They're spreading out on either side and mighty quick they'll have us between a crossfire. Yep, reckon this is it."

"Looks that way, all right," Doc Holliday agreed cheerfully. "Wonder what Hell's like, anyhow?"

"You'll find out in another five minutes or so," Morgan predicted grimly as he fired at a hint of movement among the rocks.

However, the end did not come immediately. The drygulchers were cautious, taking great care not to expose themselves as they crept slowly to right and left. They evidently figured they could afford to take their time and not risk a chance with the expert marksmen holed up behind the clump of stone.

Wyatt ducked as a bullet whistled past his ear. He fired in the direction of the shot. Another slug chipped fragments from the boulder which sheltered him. The drygulchers had almost completed their encircling movement and were getting the range.

"Guess we might as well rush them and try and take a few with us when we go," he said. He was rising to his feet when from the silent slope on his right a voice rang out like the peal of a great bell—

"There they are, boys! Up and at 'em! Don't let one get away!" Followed a clatter of hoofs and a bellow of gunfire.

Wyatt flung up his head in amazed unbelief. Tearing down the rock strewn, brush studded slope was a great black horse that leaped over boulders, swerved around bushes, looking like a dozen in one. Its tall rider was shooting with both hands and yelling at the top of his voice.

Guns blazing, Walt Slade charged down the slope at breakneck speed. He saw one of the drygulchers pitch forward on his face. A second leaped into the air and crashed to the ground. A storm of bullets buzzed around him. Then a third man went down, kicking and clawing among the rocks. The others, seized by sudden panic, rushed madly toward the thicket behind which their horses were concealed.

With a leader's instinct, Wyatt Earp acted. He leaped to his feet and rushed into the open.

"Shoot, boys! Shoot!" he roared, pulling trigger as fast as he could. Three of the best shots in Arizona lined sights with the fleeing outlaws. One went down, another, and another, and still another. The three remaining reached the horses, flung themselves into the saddles and raced west over the broken ground, slugs whistling all about them.

Walt Slade slammed his empty Colts into their holsters and jerked his Winchester from the boot. His gray eyes glanced along the sights, the big rifle spurted smoke.

A hat went flying through the air. The dying sunlight gleamed on the golden hair of its owner.

Slade lined sights again, but the fleeing outlaw swerved around a boulder, tore through a clump of brush and continued on his way. Leaning low in the saddle, an almost impossible target on his bounding horse, a tall bay, he eluded the stream of lead Slade sent after him and was quickly out of range. Slade holstered the rifle and tightened his grip on the bridle. Then he relaxed. It was no use. Shadow had already covered more than sixty miles and was in no shape for a gruelling race. And the big bay was fresh. Slade muttered a bitter oath. It appeared Murray De Spain led a charmed life. The chase must go on. Maybe next time . . .

He rode on down the slope and dismounted. Morgan Earp let out an astonished yell.

"By heavens! It's Slade!" he whooped. "Feller, am I glad to see you! Never was so glad to see anybody in my life!"

"I sure had the feel of a coal shovel in my hands," Doc Holliday remarked briskly. "Feller, if there's any little thing you might want done, like shooting three or four people or burning down the courthouse, I'm your huckleberry!"

Wyatt Earp said nothing. He strode across to Slade and held out a brown and sinewy hand.

Together they inspected the dead outlaws. Three were undoubtedly Mexican half-breeds. The other four were hard-looking white men. Wyatt Earp shook his head.

"Where in the devil do they come from?" he growled. "I never saw any of them before."

"From south of the Border, the chances are," Slade replied. "Perhaps some of them all the way from Texas."

"What I can't understand is why they ambushed us," said Wyatt.

"I think I can offer one explanation," Slade replied. "Murray De Spain has a virulent hatred for all peace officers, no matter who they are or where. Nothing pleases him more than to mow down a posse; he's done it before. There may be other reasons I don't know about. By the way, why are you fellows out here?"

Wyatt told him. Slade nodded his head thoughtfully. "There's another reason for the ambushing," he said. "Forty thousand dollars in gold and silver weighs heavy. Three horses packing it would have to travel slowly. In my opinion the robbers did not head for Tucson as you suspected they would. I'd say they headed straight south to Mexico. De Spain and the bunch deduced what a posse would very likely do and holed up here to take care of possible pursuit."

"And if it hadn't been for you they'd have done it," Wyatt declared emphatically.

Now it was also clear to Slade why the smuggler train the rancher saw had been so heavily convoyed. Part of the bunch had headed south with the train. The others had remained behind to execute the robbery and the ambuscade. It seemed De Spain was always one jump ahead of everybody.

"Well, I reckon we might as well be getting back to town," Wyatt decided. "We've done about all we can, I guess. It'll be dark in another ten minutes and there's no chance of overtaking those devils in the night. We'll pack poor Brady and Dunlap with us and send a wagon to pick up these other carcasses."

When they reached Tombstone, Slade paused to stable his tired horse while the others proceeded to the undertaker's establishment with the bodies of the slain cowboys.

As Wyatt Earp strode into the Oriental Bar, an unsavory character named Spence sidled up to him.

"Wyatt, didn't I see you bring in that blasted El Halcon?" he remarked unctuously. "The sooner that no-good range tramp stretches rope the better."

"Shut up!" roared Wyatt. "Another crack like that out of you and I'll pistol-whip you within an inch of your life! Get out of here!"

After giving Shadow a good rubdown and making sure all his wants were provided for, Slade repaired to the Oriental Bar for some much needed food. As he entered, Wyatt Earp hurried forward to greet him.

"Come on down to the end of the bar and have a drink with us before you eat," he invited. "I want you to shake hands with my brother Virgil, and with Mr. Richard Gird, one of the big men hereabouts, and some more of the boys."

Slade accepted the drink, and the praise showered upon him. After a few minutes of general conversation he sat down at a nearby table while a waiter hurried to bring him the best the house could provide. The great Mr. Gird, famous engineer and millionaire mine owner, drew Wyatt aside.

"Earp," he said, "just what the devil is he, anyhow, I wonder."

Wyatt glanced toward Slade's table. "Dick," he replied, "I'm going to say something, but I want you to keep it under your hat. If Slade takes a notion to talk, I reckon he'll do so. Otherwise I'm asking him no questions. But there's just one bunch of men I ever heard tell of with which that big feller would tie up perfect."

"Who are they?" asked Mr. Gird.

Wyatt again glanced toward the tall Hawk. "The Texas Rangers!"

Richard Gird stared at the marshal. "But, Wyatt," he protested, "a Texas Ranger doesn't pack any authority outside of Texas."

"No?" Wyatt returned dryly. "Well, a Texas Ranger went to Florida without papers, captured John Wesley Hardin, one of the toughest outlaws Texas ever knew, and brought him back to Texas. He killed one of Hardin's bunch and hogtied three more of 'em at the same time, He brought Hardin clean to Alabama on bluff and nerve before he got requisition papers for him. Hardin ended up making hair bridles for the state for twenty-five years. Theoretically he may not pack any authority outside of Texas, but actually a Texas Ranger packs plenty of authority, in one way or another, wherever he happens to be. Don't forget that, Dick, if some day you're on the run from one."

"I won't," Mr. Gird promised, and meant it.

EIGHTEEN

THOROUGHLY WORN OUT, Slade went to bed early, but not to sleep for some time. Tired as he was, he had plenty to occupy his mind. It seemed Murray De Spain continued to get the breaks. And the daring outlaw leader was doing very well by himself. His sideline of robbery had already netted him a neat sum. Slade knew that the fact he had lost seven men in the battle on the Benson road would bother De Spain but little. He could always enlist plenty of fresh recruits below the Border, at Pilares de Nacozari, Fronteras, Oputo and other places where individuals who had found the country north of the Rio Grande growing a bit too hot for comfort hung out. All along the Border were reckless adventurers of easy conscience ready and willing to join in any activities that promised profit. Renegade Texans, Arizonians, Mexicans and half-breeds with prices on their heads and holding allegiance to no nation were always eager to take advantage of any nefarious enterprise that came to hand. A few dead outlaws meant nothing to De Spain just so long as he was able to keep his own precious skin whole, which he had an uncanny ability to do.

However, his force was not a close-knit, disciplined organization such as the Brocius gang

There were a dozen men among Curly Bill's cohorts who could take over the leadership if something happened to Brocius. With De Spain's bunch it was different. Let De Spain himself pass out of the picture and the loose confederation of which he was the head would quickly fall apart and melt away.

Also, little loyalty could be looked for in such an aggregation. John Ringo, Joe Hill, Billy Clanton and others of his bunch would die for Curly Bill. Slade could not see any of De Spain's followers doing such a thing, unless it were some misguided Mexican who believed De Spain to be a true liberator, like the young fellow from Sinaloa.

All of which, Slade felt, simplified his task. He could concentrate on De Spain and if he managed to take care of the outlaw leader all he had set out to achieve would be accomplished. The two Texan peace officers murdered in Santa Helena Canyon would be avenged, and Slade was assured that without De Spain's assistance, vicious old Sebastian Cavorca would not be able to stage a revolution that would drench the Border country in blood.

Yes, that was all he had to do—corral Murray De Spain; but past performance, he wryly admitted, predicted that that would be quite a chore. But before he went to sleep he had planned his next move.

Slade spent the following day in Tombstone. It was necessary that Shadow should recuperate after the trip from Tucson. He questioned Wyatt Earp as to the most direct route to Skeleton Canyon. The marshal provided all the information he was able and asked no questions. Slade reasoned that after the disastrous encounter on the Benson road, De Spain would waste no time rejoining the smuggler train and accompanying it to Mexico, there to replace his losses before attempting another foray north of the Border.

The loaded mules would not be able to travel at high speed and Slade still hoped to overtake the train before it passed through Skeleton Canyon. What he would do if he did, he as yet did not know. He would await events and act in accordance with their development.

After another good night's rest, Slade rode out of Tombstone in the early morning. Shadow was thoroughly refreshed and appeared as eager for the chase as was his master.

Governed by what he had learned from Wyatt Earp, Slade did not follow the long and curving route of the Bisbee road. Instead he rode straight across Sulphur Springs Valley by way of little used trails and skirted the southern tip of the Chiricahuas, enabling him to finish the first lap of the journey in a single day's riding. He made camp in the shadow of the Chiricahuas and continued with the first light.

When he reached Skeleton Canyon, Slade quickly discovered evidence of the passage of a large body of horses and mules no great time before. It could be no other than the smuggler train. He rode on steadily, watchful and alert but not anticipating any untoward incident. From the signs, he knew he could not hope to overtake the train in Skeleton Canyon, but he hoped to sight it somewhere in the Animas Valley or beyond.

But when he pushed through the south mouth of the canyon, the broad valley lay deserted before his eyes. After a while he pulled up, rolled a cigarette and considered the prospect. The train was farther ahead than he had calculated.

Lounging comfortably in the saddle and smoking his cigarette, he could see the mouth of the San Luis Pass southeast across the valley. The wide gap and its environs were, as usual, swathed in purplish-blue mist that, unless it shifted before a wind, obscured objects.

As he gazed, Slade noticed what appeared to be movement in the mist. There was a change of color from the soft blueness to the whitish yellow of dust. Across the sky above the shimmering silver of a mirage surged a gigantic figure, distorted, unreal. But as he gazed the colossal form dwindled into a single horseman riding southward into the pass. Another materialized from the shadows, and another. Following was a long line of mules, the *aparejos* bulging out from their sides, more horsemen riding on either side. In utter silence they vanished into the pass. Still more riders brought up the rear. Then again the emptiness of the blue mist and the coppery sky overhead. Slade could almost believe that it was all but a mirage, reflected happenings taking place perhaps miles distant.

But he knew it wasn't so. The ghostly riders had been real. What he had seen was De Spain's smuggler train driving into Mexico. He could not hope to overtake them this side of the Border. Once again he would be on his own. The famous Silver Star on a silver circle snugged in its secret pocket meant nothing down there so far as official authority was concerned. Honest men would respect it, but that was all. He would be strictly on his own. He pinched out his cigarette, gathered up the reins and sent Shadow forward across the Animas Valley.

The last rays of the setting sun were flashing golden on the crests of the Peloncillos as Slade rode into the wide-flung jaws of the San Luis. The heavens above were filled with light, but the canyon ahead was a curdling of shadows, ominous shadows that seemed to motion to him to turn back while there was yet time. He rode on.

He camped in the pass that night, a most wild and desolate spot. The light of his fire flickered on great ruddy ribs of rock which towered overhead, and on the dark green twisted pines and junipers that appeared to writhe in torment.

Like Skeleton Canyon, the San Luis had every right to be haunted. Its stones were black with dried blood. Here, not long before, Curly Bill and his outlaws had killed fourteen Mexicans in the course of a widelooping foray. An aftermath of those killings had been the death of ferocious Old Man Clanton and four others of Curly Bill's followers in Guadalupe Canyon, mowed down by dark-faced avengers from below the Line.

The following morning Slade rode out of the pass. Before him lay the Playas Valley and Mexico. And somewhere down here amid the mountains and valleys was the trail of Murray De Spain.

Slade reasoned that the smuggler train would very likely swing slightly westward through the Casas Grandes to Pilares de Nacozari, where the loads of contraband would be rerouted to various points in the interior. And it was not improbable that De Spain would remain in Pilares de Nacozari for a while, although he might possibly continue south to Cumpas. At any rate he should be found somewhere along the Rio Nacozari; the whole section was a favorite hangout for Border raiders. Slade rode on.

A trail ran through the San Luis, a well-travelled trail that pursued its way down the southern slopes. Some miles farther on it swerved to enter a broad valley that trended south by slightly west. It led, Slade was confident, to Pilares de Nacozari, doubtless with branches to the south and east. Several miles inside the valley he came to a small village which boasted a *cantina* that was spotlessly clean and surprisingly large for so tiny a settlement. It was run by a plump and jolly and very pretty *señora* who answered Slade's fluent Spanish with a warm smile and a flash of her dark eyes.

She seemed to find this tall young *señor* from the north to her liking, for she sat at table with him while he ate the excellent food she had prepared with her own capable hands.

"Your place is large and looks prosperous," Slade commented, glancing about. "Are there other *pueblos* nearby?"

"None," she replied, "but many men ride this way, wild young men from the north who are said to be *muy malo hombres*. Perhaps they are very bad men, but to us of the village they are kindly and courteous. They eat hugely, drink much and pay well, dance with the *señoritas* and sing. I hear that they prey on the great *haciendas* to the south. Doubtless it is so, for often in the nighttimes we hear the hoofs of horses travelling swiftly, and the bleating of many *ganado* also travelling swiftly. Then later, at times, we hear other men ride past, men who curse, and belabor their *caballos*. The horses snort angrily and sometimes squeal and their hoofs drum the ground."

She paused to laugh melodiously, as if she found the irate pursuit of the rustlers splitting the wind for north of the Border vastly amusing. "At times it is the other way around," she added. "At times the *ganado* come rushing down from the north with the horsemen flogging them on. Then later will come cursing men who ride south hot on their trail. But after a while they mostly ride back this way, empty-handed but jovial. They pause to drink my wine and make the joke over their fruitless ride. It is all good fun, *si*?"

"Sometimes," Slade smiled, "but sometimes it is a serious business if those behind catch up with those in front."

"That is so," she agreed, "but men must shed blood now and then if they are to be happy, and risk their own blood. Men are strange creatures."

"Women are at times a bit puzzling, too," Slade chuckled.

The dark, laughing eyes met his. "But would you have them otherwise?" she asked. "If men always knew what women are thinking, it would be a lonely world—for women."

This time it was Slade who laughed aloud. He felt that this experienced little *señora* had stated the case precisely.

"Have many ridden this way of late?" he asked casually.

However, his casualness did not fool her in the least, as he quickly realized.

"To most who ask I would answer no," she replied. "But to one whose eyes are kindness and whose heart is clean I may speak only truth. Last night, an hour after the dark had fallen, many men passed this way. Men who drove laden mules. Were they indeed *muy malo hombres*?"

"Yes," Slade said, "they were truly very bad men."

"So I thought," she nodded. "Some paused here to drink, and they were uneasy men to traffic with. There was one especially, a man tall and nobly formed. On his face rested much beauty and his hair was like to the gold of the sunshine, but there was no sunshine in his eyes. They were the eyes of the *gato*, the great tiger-lion of the forests. I crossed myself when his gaze rested upon me and murmured a prayer that the Virgin might guard me from evil."

She paused, then asked, "Do you ride after those men, tall *señor*?"

"Truth begets truth," Slade answered. "I do."

"Now may God and His saints preserve you from evil," she said earnestly.

NINETEEN

SLADE RENEWED HIS SUPPLY OF PROVISIONS, said good-bye to the friendly *señora* and rode on. He was elated to learn that he had guessed right, that De Spain had really accompanied the smuggler train south. But it was farther ahead than he had thought, for it appeared that De Spain had ordered forced marches and was giving men and animals scant time to rest on the way, something which led Slade to believe that the outlaw had some other project in mind and was impatient to put it into execution.

All day he rode at a steady pace. The valley, which had developed a distinctly westward trend, was for the most part heavily grown with chaparral through which the trail wound, often affording visibility of only a few yards.

It was ticklish work, for he never knew what a bend in the trail would reveal or what he might meet coming around the next turn. His nerves grew taut with the unceasing suspense, his eyes ached from his constant searching of the terrain ahead. His hearing, spurred by an overactive imagination, began playing tricks. The note of a bird in the bushes became the faint jingle of bridle irons; the scuffle of some little animal scurrying through the growth was the soft beat of stealthily approaching hoofs held in by an alert rider with a gun in his hand and ready to open fire at anyone coming down from the north. Slade swore at himself and tried to subdue the rising tension that was making him jumpy. His nervousness communicated to his horse, and Shadow was ready to shy at the glint of a sunbeam penetrating the interlacing of branches overhead. Slade felt he would welcome anything that would serve to break the intolerable monotony of apprehension.

He breathed a sigh of relief when, an hour or so before sunset, the valley opened into another and much wider valley running at right angles to the first. Here was rolling land, sparsely grown, with occasional low hills. The range of his vision was greatly increased and the opportunity to relax a little was very welcome.

Shadow toiled up a long rise, cantered briskly down the opposite side and crossed a couple of miles of level ground before tackling another and even longer slope. The lower edge of the sun was touching the western hilltops when he reached the crest. Slade pulled him to a halt and leaned forward eagerly.

Far in the distance he could see a swarthy dust cloud rising against the evening sky and rolling steadily forward. Only a herd of cattle or a large number of other hoofed animals could kick up such a fog. It was reasonable to believe that the smuggler train was responsible.

For some minutes he sat studying the advancing cloud, trying to estimate the speed at which the train was travelling, hoping to see the sudden settling that would indicate the outlaws were halting to make camp for the night. Now that he had found the darn thing, he didn't know what to do with it. He could hardly charge the whole gang singlehanded. Also, his interest was centered on Murray De Spain. The others were small fry and of little account.

The dust cloud rolled on. Apparently De Spain was bent on taking advantage of the last minute of daylight. However, Slade thought it unlikely that he would continue after dark. According to what the *señora* said, he had made a late camp the night before, and there was a limit to what the laden mules could endure. Slade spoke to Shadow and rode down the slope.

Overhead the sky flamed gold and rose, dulled to steely gray. The stars came out. The dusk deepened and night birds uttered their calls. Still Slade rode steadily at a good pace. The train was many miles ahead and he desired to cut down the distance as much as seemed practicable. When morning came and the smugglers resumed their southward trek he wanted to be close enough to observe their movements and possibly forsee their intentions.

Finally he pulled up where a little stream babbled across the trail. It would be foolhardy and would gain him nothing to approach the camp at night. Besides, Shadow wanted rest and he might need everything the big black had to give before another day drew to a close. The good *señora* had insisted that he take along some cooked food and thanks to her foresight he did not go hungry even though he dared not risk lighting a fire.

"A horse without its fodder and a man without his meat are good for little," she had said. "And you, tall *señor*, cannot thrive on grass."

Slade's desire was to capture De Spain and rush him across the Border to Arizona, where he would have no difficulty obtaining extradition papers for him back to Texas.

A hazardous undertaking, on the face of it well nigh impossible, but he had drawn cards in the game and felt he had to play the hand out. He went to sleep with an easy mind, content to let events develop as they would and perhaps provide opportunity.

Dawn found him in the saddle, much refreshed by his night's rest and ready for anything. A couple of miles below where he made his camp, one of the low hills started up from the valley floor. Here the little stream which paralleled the trail divided to flow around this natural barrier. On either side it widened out to form wide stretches of marsh. To avoid the bog, the trail climbed upward across the east shoulder of the hill. Slade sent Shadow up the winding slant at an easy pace. The sun was above the horizon and shining brightly, bathing the trail in brilliant light that caused every rock and clump of brush to stand out in stark detail. The crest of the rise was asmolder with a golden glow.

Slade reached the crest, rode over it. Then he abruptly jerked Shadow to a halt and backed him down the north slope. Ahead, less than two miles distant and seeming nearer in the flood of light was the smuggler train wending its way south. Apparently the outlaws had broken camp late; anyhow they were much nearer than Slade had anticipated.

With only his head showing above the crest, Slade studied the train and the vista beyond. The mules were travelling at a steady pace with nearly a dozen outriders pacing before, behind and on either side. A thousand yards or so ahead of where the laden animals trudged along, the whole character of the country changed. The rolling land, gentle slopes and rounded hills were replaced by a jumble of rugged buttes, tall chimney rocks and towering cliffs, interspersed by dense chaparral. Into this badland the trail flowed.

It was out of the question at this moment to ride down the slope and across the intervening level land, so Slade settled himself comfortably in the saddle and rolled a cigarette. He watched the last mule vanish into the gloom of the wild terrain ahead, the drag riders following.

However, he still made no move. He wanted the train to get well ahead before pursuing it through the broken country. To do otherwise would be taking a needless risk. He would be clearly outlined as he rode down the slope and across the level and from some point in there visibility might be good. He allowed nearly an hour to elapse before he sent Shadow forward again.

Slade was not altogether easy in his mind. He rather doubted if the naked eye would have spotted his brief appearance on the crest, if the smugglers were keeping a watch on their back trail, which was probable. But the wily De Spain, who missed no bets, might employ mechanical means to supplement his vision. Slade recalled Wyatt Earp mentioning that from his commanding hilltop stronghold in the San Pedro Valley, Old Man Clanton used to sweep the valley with a pair of field glasses up and down for seventy-five miles and appraise every man on horseback, every bunch of cattle, every stagecoach. Murray De Spain might well utilize a similar device, and if he had been scanning the back trail at the moment, he would not only have noted the horseman riding over the hill crest but would quite likely have been able to establish his identity also.

Well, that was a chance he would have to take.

He rode on down the slope and across the wide level space.

As he neared the broken ground, he realized that his gaze could follow the trail for some distance. For more than a mile it ran arrow-straight before curving around a tall butte. No chance for an ambush this side of the bend.

Approaching the turn he rode warily, with every sense tensely alert. With Shadow proceeding at a slow walk he rounded it without untoward incident. Again the trail stretched ahead for some distance. Nothing was in sight and no sound reached his ears. He observed that birds fluttering around the thickets gave no indication of alarm. He rode on, negotiated another turn. It began to look as if his fears were groundless, that he had not been spotted topping the rise. He quickened Shadow's pace a little and relaxed somewhat. Another bend loomed, with dense thickets flanking it on either side. He eyed it with mild interest; doubtless the smuggler train was miles ahead.

It was the sudden upward thrust of a jay that saved him. The beautiful blue bird came flitting toward the bend at right-angles to the trail. Suddenly it screamed with alarm and shot straight up in the air, whisked about and streaked back the way it had come. Slade jerked Shadow to a halt. His eyes flickered over the belt of growth and sensed rather than saw movement. Movement and the quick gleam of sunlight on shifted metal. He whirled Shadow on a dime.

"Trail!" his voice rang out.

The great horse bounded forward on the back track. From the growth flanking the trail came an angry yell, then a fusillade of shots. Slade bent low in the saddle as bullets buzzed past. He did not turn his head but gave his attention to getting every fraction of speed from the tall black. Not even when he heard the clash of irons on the hard surface of the trail did he look back. He had ridden into an ambush and it was up to him to put distance between him and the drygulchers without delay.

The bullets continued to come, but a man on the back of a bounding horse is a poor target for another man on another speeding cayuse. Slade was untouched and he knew he was drawing away from the pursuit. Drawing away, but very slowly; the pursuers were well mounted. He risked a glance over his shoulder. There were six of them, just careening around a bend. Foremost was a tall man mounted on a splendid bay. Slade did not need two glances to assure him that it was none other than Murray De Spain. A bullet fanned his cheek and he turned back to the front and urged Shadow to greater speed.

Slade had every faith in Shadow's speed and endurance, but the big black had had a hard week, and the going was bad for such reckless speed. At any instant a loose stone rolling under a downward plunging hoof, a slight washout, a rodent's burrow might spell disaster. A fall would be fatal, a bad sprain only more slowly so.

Behind, the gunfire had stopped. He had been able to gain enough to make anything like accurate shooting impossible. The outlaws, realizing this, had ceased to waste ammunition and had settled themselves for a long and gruelling chase. Slade knew that Murray De Spain would never give up so long as his horse was able to plant one foot in front of another or he was hopelessly outdistanced. He was out to do away with his hated enemy once and for all.

Slade talked quietly to Shadow, eased off a little, until he was just holding the distance he had gained; he must conserve the horse's strength as much as possible.

A few minutes later he glanced back again and saw that while he was holding his own against the main body of the pursuit, he was not holding it against De Spain. The tall bay was a magnificent animal and the outlaw leader was gaining. And while doing so he had pulled away from his followers until he was riding more than a hundred yards to the front of them.

Slade again spoke to Shadow, and again the black horse lengthened his stride. Slade gauged his speed with the greatest nicety, endeavoring to hold De Spain to a dead heat. He was doing it and all the while De Spain was drawing farther and farther away from his followers. Now the hundred yards had increased to better than two.

And in Walt Slade's mind a daring plan was taking form. It would be an insanely reckless gamble with death, but he believed it had at least an outside chance to succeed.

He reached the straight stretch of trail before the more open country to the north. As he flashed out from the jumble of rocks he glanced over his shoulder.

De Spain had gained a little, but in so doing he had increased the distance between himself and the others to nearly four hundred yards. Slade wondered if he realized how much he had detached himself from his men. Perhaps he didn't, and then perhaps he didn't give a hang. No matter what he might be, Murray De Spain feared no man and was supremely confident in his own prowess. At any rate he continued to ride with unabated speed, his whole interest centered on his quarry, the man he hated, the man who had thwarted him again and again and who clung like a very nemesis to his trail. Now without a doubt his dark spirit exulted: he was no longer the pursued but the pursuer; and slowly but surely he was gaining. Soon he would thunder in for the kill.

At least Slade hoped that was what he thought and would continue to for a while. The success of his plan depended on De Spain in the excitement of the chase throwing caution to the winds.

"It's showdown, horse," he told Shadow. "Either I'm going to accomplish what I came down here to do or stay here forever."

Across the open flat the grim race continued, with De Spain steadily drawing away from his men who were quirting their horses in a vain attempt to catch up with their leader. Now they were a good six hundred yards behind the flying bay. Slade glanced back as Shadow breasted the slope where the trail wound over the shoulder of hill. They would close the distance somewhat with both horses toiling up the hill trail, but he did not think it would be enough to matter greatly. He gave his attention to riding, bending low in the saddle, talking soothingly to his mount. Shadow was blowing a little but he still showed no signs of faltering.

De Spain, still on the level ground, gained enough to chance a shot. The bullet whistled past Slade, was followed by another that came closer. But when the bay tackled the slope, De Spain ceased firing. Slade had a notion the brown horse was beginning to feel the effects of his prodigious efforts; it no longer mattered, the end, one way or another, was close at hand.

Shadow reached the crest of the rise, flashed over it and sped down the opposite sag, with Slade fighting to halt him. Fifty yards down the slope he skittered to a stop, blowing and snorting. Slade slid his Winchester from the saddle boot and dropped to the ground. He turned, faced the crest that glowed against the sky and waited, the rifle cocked and ready.

TWENTY

THE PURSUING OUTLAW LOOMED GIGANTIC in the golden sunlight as he topped the rise and Slade opened fire as fast as he could pull trigger. The ejection lever was a flashing blur; did a cartridge jam it would shatter like matchwood.

There was little to shoot at; De Spain, hunched behind his horse's neck, presented the smallest target possible, and he was firing with both hands. Slade felt the wind of passing slugs, the jerk of one that ripped through his sleeve. He paid the whining lead no mind and concentrated his every faculty on the horseman charging toward him.

A terrific blow on the calf of his left leg hurled him sideways and almost off his feet. At the same instant another bullet grazed his forehead, sending blood streaming down his face, rendering him sick and dizzy with the shock. He fired again and again, felt himself going. In another instant he would fall, and that would be the end. Grimly resting all his weight on his sound leg, he lined sights with De Spain and squeezed the trigger. Only a sharp click of the firing pin on an exploded cartridge followed. Reeling, dizzy, his eyes blinded by blood and pain, he dropped the empty rifle and went for his Colts. The earth was heaving under his feet, the heavens reeling and shivering.

Then abruptly he stiffened. The tall bay horse was rearing high under the spasmodic pull of dying hands, and between the heaving earth and the reeling sky, Murray De Spain swayed sideways in his saddle, blood gushing from his mouth and crimsoning his shirt front. He toppled from the hull and fell, striking the ground with a muffled thud, to lie motionless.

Slade scooped up the fallen rifle, limped and floundered to his horse. After vain attempts he managed to crawl into the saddle and sheath the Winchester just as Murray De Spain's followers stormed over the crest. Twisting in the saddle he drew his guns and fired blindly with both hands, again and again.

Suddenly he realized he was shooting at thin air. The outlaws, seized with panic, had scurried back down the slope, leaving two of their number prone in the dust of the trail. Slade faced to the front.

"Trail, Shadow, trail!" he gasped.

The great black shot forward, his irons drumming the ground. Down the long and winding slope he careened. As he reached the level ground, guns cracked behind and again Slade heard the lethal whisper of passing lead. But Shadow was going like the wind and the shooting quickly ceased. Glancing back, Slade saw that the outlaws were grouped around their fallen leader. If he could manage to stay in the saddle, there was little chance that they would overtake him even if they attempted to do so.

But he was in a very bad way. His wounded leg throbbed and burned and his head was one vast ache. Red and purple bands of light came and went before his eyes, his muscles seemed turning to water and the deadly lethargy that threatened to engulf him told that he had already lost a great deal of blood. His breathing was labored and as he attempted to tighten his grip on the reins, his hands pawed ineffectually.

Still he grimly refused to give in. To do so would very likely prove fatal. The outlaws, sensing that he was wounded and weak, might continue the pursuit, and there might be others following on the trail with fresh horses. Quite probably De Spain had thought of that also; it appeared he thought of everything.

Mile after mile sped past under Shadow's tireless hoofs. In the deepening twilight the mouth of the bush grown valley was reached. Slade dimly realized the fact, enough so to turn Shadow's head east. Maybe he had enough left to make it to the little *señora*'s *cantina* near the eastern end of the valley. He leaned forward, twined his fingers in Shadow's coarse mane and grimly held on, twisting his spurs against the stirrup straps, although every movement of his bullet-torn leg was an agony.

Walt Slade remembered very little of that terrible ride. He was vaguely conscious of the drumming of Shadow's irons on the hard soil, of a constant stream of bristling chaparral flickering past in the starlight, of bushes that seemed to writhe and twist with malevolent movement, of trees that were not trees but grisly spectres reaching out gnarled arms and clutching hands.

And still the great black horse sped on. He was blowing now, his breath coming in sobbing gasps, his sides heaving. His nostrils were flaring, his eyes gorged with blood. But on he sped, needing no whip to goad him into giving his all.

Lights flashed ahead and Slade realized he had reached the village near the valley mouth. The building which housed the *cantina* loomed before him. He pulled back feebly on the reins.

"Hold it, feller, hold it!" he croaked.

Shadow jolted to a sobbing halt before the open door through which poured a bar of golden light. He stood with hanging head and legs widespread as Slade staggered to the door.

There was a cry inside the *cantina*, then a babble of excited voices and a patter of swift light steps. The little *señora* cried out again as she recognized him.

"My horse," Slade panted. "Look after him, somebody."

"We will," promised the *señora.* "Come! Help me, Manuel."

Dazed, Slade realized that strong arms were around him, supporting him, guiding his faltering steps. He was led into a lighted room and gently eased upon a bed. A door was closed to shut out the noise and he was deftly undressed. He sensed that the little *señora* was working over his wounds, her touch amazingly gentle, murmuring soft Spanish the while. A glass was held to his lips. Mechanically he swallowed the contents. A delicious warmth and a sense of well-being suffused him. The forms and faces of those hovering over him grew hazy and he knew no more.

When Slade awakened, sunlight was streaming across the bed. By the open window lounged a tall young Mexican smoking a cigarette. He turned to reveal gay, laughing dark eyes that were the *señora*'s in a masculine face.

"*Buenos dias*!" he greeted warmly, then reverted to the precise English of the mission-taught Mexican. "So you awake? *Madrecita* insisted that I with you remain till you did. I will summon her."

He left the room and a few minutes later the little *señora* bustled in, her eyes bright with gladness.

"Ha!" she exclaimed. "You live! Which is more than I had hoped for at one time. There was death in your face when you arrived here. Now I will prepare food. You are hungry, *si*? Men are always hungry, even in the throes of love or at the point of death. And never are they content unless they are shedding blood. You lost much of your own. First let me examine the wound in your leg. Manuel, bring warm water and cloths."

With her deft, gentle touch she undid the bandages she had applied the night before. A brief examination and she nodded with satisfaction. "It mends," she said. "Your blood, like your heart, is clean. You will take no lasting harm save for the scars that must remain. There, that is finished. Do not move it suddenly and you must remain in bed for another day lest you start the bleeding a-fresh. Now your face. Warm water and a cloth will care for that."

"And I could use soap and a razor," Slade added.

"Both you shall have after you have eaten," she promised. "And men call women vain! If a whisker blues their jowls it must be removed at once."

She pattered out to return soon with a savory breakfast which she watched him eat with pleasure, insisting on cutting the meat for him and assisting him in every way possible.

"Keep this up and I'll never leave," he threatened.

"Were I but twenty years younger, here you would remain," she declared.

"If you were twenty years younger, I could only remain as your father," he returned gallantly.

She trilled girlish laughter. "It is sin to make jest of the old," she smiled, and looked anything but old enough to be the mother of the stalwart Manuel who lounged nearby wearing an amused grin.

In deference to the *señora*'s insistence, Slade remained three days at the *cantina.* Manuel loitered about, watching the trail to the west, a Sharps buffalo gun ready to hand. However, Slade had little fear that the outlaws would come looking for him. With De Spain dead, the whole loosely formed organization would quickly fall apart.

"*Hasta luego*—till we meet again—" he told his kindly hostess as he mounted Shadow, now in the best of condition. "I think I can say with truth that I owe my life to you. I don't believe I'd have lasted to the Border. Someday I'll ride back this way, in better times."

Despite an occasional pang that shot through his healing leg, Walt Slade was in a satisfied and complacent mood. Things had worked out a lot better than he had at one time expected. He had triumphed in his long feud with the outlaw chief and he was confident that without De Spain's help and guidance, old Sebastian Cavorca would not be able to stage a Border rising. He looked forward to Texas with pleasant anticipation and wondered what fresh chore Captain McNelty would have lined up for him by the time he got back to the Post. With a light heart and laughter in his eyes, he rode north.

Slade reached Tombstone without misadventure; he had decided to visit the silver city and say good-bye to Wyatt Earp before riding east.

"See you have a mark or two to show for your trip," commented the marshal. "Did you see De Spain?"

"Yes," Slade replied briefly.

"Where is he now?"

"In Mexico, and he'll stay there," Slade answered. "You don't need to worry about De Spain anymore."

"So I gather," the marshal returned dryly. "Fact is, I figured that when you rode south last week. Going to leave us now?"

"Yes," Slade answered, "I'm riding."

"I'm riding up to Benson myself," observed Wyatt. "Anything I can do for you before I go?"

"Yes," Slade accepted the offer, "you can do something for me when you reach Benson, if you don't mind. I'd like you to send a telegram for me."

Wyatt procured paper and pen and Slade

wrote a brief message addressed to Captain Jim McNelty, Ranger Post Headquarters. He handed it to the marshal, who did not look at all surprised as he read it.

> Heading back to Texas. It was finished down Mexico way!

Books are produced in the United States using U.S.-based materials

Books are printed using a revolutionary new process called THINKtech™ that lowers energy usage by 70% and increases overall quality

Books are durable and flexible because of Smyth-sewing

Paper is sourced using environmentally responsible foresting methods and the paper is acid-free

Center Point Large Print
600 Brooks Road / PO Box 1
Thorndike, ME 04986-0001 USA

(207) 568-3717

US & Canada:
1 800 929-9108
www.centerpointlargeprint.com